CATCH TO A RAT

Published under licence by Brown Dog Books and
The Self-Publishing Partnership, 7 Green Park Station, Bath BA1 1JB

www.selfpublishingpartnership.co.uk

ISBN printed book: 978-1-83952-127-0
ISBN e-book: 978-1-83952-128-7

Cover design by Earl B Henry
Internal design by Andrew Easton

Printed and bound in the UK

This book is printed on FSC certified paper

TO CATCH
A RAT

A NOVEL BY

EARL B HENRY

BROWN
DOG
BOOKS

CHAPTER 1

THE CASINO DEBTS

On the 1st of July 2005, Drick E Crawford left his five-bedroom house in Greenwich, London, for his monthly gambling trip to Soames Casino in Manchester city. For many months Drick had run up debts of about £3 million in different Grosvenor casinos and hotels. Everyone knew Drick: he always said money is no problem, and every time he was asked to pay his bills Drick would say, "Put it on my books, man. Furthermore, do you know who I am? My name is Drick E Crawford and don't forget that." The term 'put it on my books' means when they place all your debts and store them for future payments.

They allowed him to run up a large bill because he had his own company. But now he had exceeded his limits.

That day, as Drick entered the Soames Casino, he was greeted by four security officers and a manager who walked up to him and escorted him to an office in the back of the casino. They told him to sit down. He became very afraid and was sweating, then he panicked and stated, "I know some significant people, and they will be furious if I am hurt." This made the manager very angry. The manager then questioned Drick whether he would be able to make a payment on his debts. He muttered, "Soon," but that answer was not satisfactory for the manager. On the account of this, the manager declared, "You have two weeks to pay us," then they took Drick's picture and placed it on the casino's computer's suspending archives. Drick began to plead, saying that his diabetes was not allowing him to make plenty of money because he was in hospital for weeks, and a company called Fibo Ltd owed him some money. He explained that he had done some music videos for them. Drick claimed that as soon as he received the money, all his debts would be paid. The manager said, "I will be suspending you from our casinos and hotels."

Then the manager and the four security officers escorted Drick out of Grosvenor Casino. As Drick was leaving, the manager explained to him:

"When you complete payment of your debts, you will be allowed back into the casinos." On account of this, he was forced to cancel his gambling trip and return to London. Drick returned to his family who had no idea about his gambling habits. When his wife inquired how was his business trip, he responded, "It was busy and I had to sign many music contracts in Manchester." He was CEO of his company, which was called Drickbo Ltd, and they were a large music video company based in Wembley.

A few weeks went by, then Drick got a call from the Scotland Yard Police Fraudsters Department. A Detective Inspector named Earl Killhill called his home and left a message on his answering machine, saying he would like to speak to Mr. Drick E Crawford. Mr. Killhill explained that he would like to make an appointment to meet him.

Later that day he got another call from a man with a Russian accent: he stated his name was Radovan Bloodmic, and he also left a message on the answering machine, asking Drick to contact him soon as possible, because he worked for a Russian debt collecting agency.

Mr. Bloodmic explained in the message that he would be flying into the country to see him, because the debt had been bought from Soames Casinos by the Russian debt collection agency which is owned by the Russian mafia. Radovan mentioned on the phone that a collector's fee of £2 million would be added to the £3 million. So Drick now owed £5 million in debt to the Russian debt collection agency, and not Soames Casinos.

Because of the large amount of money that was to be collected, that is the reason why they chose Radovan Bloodmic, a former KGB general-turned-Russian debt collector. He stated he was paid a very large sum of money to fly in from Russia to collect the debt that was bought by his bosses' company. When Drick got home he listened to his answering machine messages, but he was not aware of the drastic way his life was about to change.

So Mr. Bloodmic arrived and went directly to the casino to get Drick's details. On the 2nd of July, Drick awoke early at about 6.30 and began to do his exercises; then he helped his wife get their son ready for school. He made breakfast for his family and was mowing the lawns before he left for work.

The phone rang at about 7.45. Drick turned and ran into the house. As he picked up the phone, his face turned pale immediately because a voice in a Russian accent said, "Is this Mr. Drick E Crawford?"

Drick replied, "Yes, and who are you?"

The voice said, "My name is Radovan Bloodmic. I called and left a message on your house phone."

Mr. Bloodmic explained again that he was an agent hired by his boss to collect the money for the casino's debt, and the amount was £5 million. Drick, with a very unusual look on his face, shouted, "What!? 5 million? I thought it was 3 million." Mr. Bloodmic explained that 2 million was his collection fee.

Mr. Radovan Bloodmic stated that he would be coming to Drick's office in Wembley, on the 7th of July at about 2.00 pm. Drick responded. "Okay, I will meet you there," but he couldn't believe his ears, and his brain started to work overtime. He began to think where was he going to find £5 million? His company was only worth about £4 million. Drick returned to the yard and finished mowing the lawns. He was mowing for about five minutes when the phone rang again.

Drick's wife Seri answered and shouted out of the window, saying, "The phone is for you."

Drick muttered in a very nervous voice, "Who is it, Seri?"

Seri replied, "It is a Scotland Yard detective, love." Drick slowly walked to the house, trying to look calm so that his wife would not see his nervousness.

He took the phone from Seri and said, "Hello, this is Drick E Crawford." The person on the phone spoke:

"This is Detective Inspector Earl Killhill. I am investigating a tax evasion claim." Mr. Killhill said that he was coming to see Drick at his office at about 2.30 pm on the 8th of July. Drick replied,

"No problem, I will meet you there." He was even more nervous, and he hung up the phone and went to the back of the house to finish mowing the lawns. After he had finished, he sat on the lawn looking to the sky for divine intervention. Drick remembered he had an 11 am meeting at Wembley Stadium, so he got up and went into the bathroom and got showered and dressed. Before leaving for work, Drick wrote on a notepad the names of the detective and the time of the appointment and the name of the debt collector and the time of the appointment and placed it into his pocket. He got showered and left the house to catch his train for work in Wembley.

CHAPTER 2

ANSWERING QUESTIONS

Drick got off his train at Wembley Central station. After looking at his watch, he saw there was time to buy himself a coffee. He entered the Moon-Cups coffee shop and bought himself two cups of coffee and a doughnut. At that moment he was about to exit the coffee shop, when he ran into his friend Dean Sanders.

"How are you?" he asked. "I haven't seen you for about a week, and how are your family?"

Drick responded. "My family is fine," then he told him about the two phone calls he had received a few days ago.

He uttered, "Dean, today is the worst day of my life. If I knew how to disappear I would have done it."

Dean responded. "Don't be stupid, Drick, you have to face your problems."

Drick muttered, "With problems as large as mine I need to disappear, yet my worries are not as much about the Detective Inspector Earl Killhill, but the Russian debt collector Radovan Bloodmic: he makes me extremely nervous. They said he was an ex-KGB general-turned-mafia. Now he's a debt collector."

Dean replied, "Oh my friend, you sound like you're in real trouble."

Drick explained to Dean: "I read about the Russian mafia, and they are a very nasty piece of work. I heard they cut off your bodyparts and send them to your family while you're still alive."

Dean questioned, "Drick, how much money do you owe them?"

Drick whispered, "£5 million."

Dean shouted, "What!?" Drick told him to be quiet.

"Five million," he repeated.

Thus Drick explained that he really owed three million. But the debt collector has added two million for the collection fees. Dean rose from his seat and said, "Let's go back to the office. Furthermore, they can't do that."

Their offices were situated five minutes from the coffee shop, with Drick's office on the ground floor. So they both left the coffee shop and went back to their offices.

Drick yelled, "Oh no, I forgot my doughnut! I'm going back to the shop to collect it."

Dean muttered, "Okay," and continued to his office. As Drick stepped out of the office into the car park, a gentleman walked up to him and said, "Drick E Crawford?"

Drick answered, "Yes, who would like to know?"

The gentleman said, "I am Detective Inspector Earl Killhill, and I came here to have a word with you please."

Then he pointed to a BMW 5 Series Jeep: this caused Drick to become extremely tense and start sweating.

The detective added, "Please can you get into the back?" Drick opened the back door of the Jeep and sat on the back seat. To his horror he realised that there was no way he could open the door from inside. Then Detective Killhill came round to the passenger side door and entered the back.

"What's this about?" asked Drick, as if he was oblivious to what the detective was saying to him.

"You know what this is about: I'm here to speak to you concerning your tax evasion."

Drick responded. "Tax evasion? I have paid all my taxes, and my accountant said he filed all my taxes for last year."

The detective replied, "No taxes were filed and you owe the government £2 million now, so we need a down payment of £400,000."

Drick yelled, "Where am I going to find £400,000!? Furthermore, I don't have that type of money!"

The detective replied, "That's not my problem, hence I'll be speaking to you soon."

He then pressed a remote control button he had in this pocket, and the Jeep doors opened and Drick got out. "Bye, for now," declared the detective, as he got into his driver's seat and drove off. Drick began feeling very ill, as he made a few steps towards his office.

He felt as if someone was watching him. Drick looked around sharply, but he couldn't see anyone, as he made a few steps towards his office. A gentleman, about 6 feet 5 inches tall, stepped in front of him and spoke.

"Drick E Crawford?"

Drick replied, "Yes, I am Mr. Crawford."

The gentleman explained his name was Radovan Bloodmic and

he came to speak to him. Drick thought how life could be so hard, because two of his biggest enemies had seen him within the space of 10 minutes.

Drick continued. "I was not expecting you today."

Radovan replied, "I had some free time and I was in the area, because I came all the way from Russia to see you and collect my money. I left a message on your phone but you did not return my call, so I came here to meet you. As I explained, the sum will be £5 million: our collection fee is £2 million. That's what my boss stated, and that's what I will be collecting in the next three weeks. Please don't mess with me or else you know what we can do to you." He jumped into the back of a tinted-out Mercedes Jeep and then drove off.

Drick was now terrified and he was shaking as if he was hit by a magnitude 10 earthquake. Drick smiled and thought, 'I'll file for bankruptcy against the government, but that cannot pay the Russian debt collector.' So he became despondent instantly.

Life is like a wave: it goes up, and it comes down, but Drick's life seemed to be going down and down and down, and no way up. Drick strolled back into the building, shaking.

A member of staff noticed him and asked, "Are you okay?"

He replied, "Yes, just have a bit of a problem."

Then he went upstairs to the Dean's office and remarked, "Dean, you will not believe what has just happened to me in the last 20 minutes, after I went back to get my doughnut. Both of them came after me: the detective and the Russian mafia."

Dean stood in horror and declared, "What, you're joking?"

Drick responded, "No, I am not. Both of them met me in the car park: it was as if they were sitting there waiting and watching us when we came back from the cafe."

Drick remarked, "I feel as if I owe the world money."

Dean replied, "That has to be a very crazy feeling: you know you have to sort it out. Pay someone some instalments."

Drick muttered, "The Russians don't want any instalments, they want £5 million in full. I think I will have to sell both of my houses and some of my studios. I have two girlfriends and one wife. You think I could sell them on eBay?"

"Don't be stupid," stated Dean, "you can't sell your wife. If you want to sell your wife, then sell yourself on eBay. That was not a nice thing to say about your wife, the mother of your kid."

"I was joking," replied Drick.

"You can't be joking in times like these: people will be trying to kill you and your family!" shouted Dean.

Drick thought, 'I'm being asked too many questions, and I'm not feeling well,' so he cancelled all of his appointments for the day and went home early to sleep.

CHAPTER 3

THE TRAIN JOURNEY

Drick awoke about 5 in the morning, and did his usual martial arts exercises. Afterwards he went and had a bath after his workout, so he could be ready for his morning meeting. He wasn't feeling well that morning because of his diabetes, and his blood sugars seemed to be very high. But he was eager to get to his early morning meeting. Next he rushed out of the house forgetting his insulin pen. He was on his way to the train station when he realised his feet were getting cold, and this meant his blood sugar levels were climbing.

Drick reached into his pocket for his injection pen but it was not there; he began frantically searching the other pockets in his clothing. Next he searched his bag: there was no injection pen, hence he realised he had left it at home. Drick was not happy because he was very late, and had to return home for his injection pen. As Drick walked into the house, he shouted, "Oh, no!" Not only did he leave his injection pen, but he also forgot his workplace pass: both of them were on the table. Hence he grabbed them quickly and hurried back to catch the train. In the haste, trying to catch the train, he accidentally walked past his newspaper shop, then quickly ran back and got himself his daily newspaper, the *Financial Times*.

Finally he ran and jumped on the train at Greenwich station. There was a packed train with early morning commuters going to work: some people smelled great, and some people did not.

Drick was on his way to Wembley. Drick's journey was from Greenwich station to Bank station, changing to the Central line at Oxford Circus, then proceeding on the Bakerloo line for Wembley Central. As Drick got into the train, he began feeling dizzy, so a pregnant lady got up and gave her seat to him as he sat down.

He felt for his diabetic injection pen in his pocket and injected himself.

When he looked up everyone, and everything, was blurred, then in about 15 seconds it all cleared. He arrived at Oxford Circus station. Drick slowly walked to the Bakerloo line. The distance seemed to be four times longer. As he got into the train and sat down, Drick remembered that he had a sandwich in his bag, so he ate the sandwich and right away began feeling well. He looked around and started chatting to a pretty young lady who was sitting near him. He asked her where she was going.

She said, "I'm going to work."

He boasted that he was a millionaire and was going to sign a huge contract that day. Drick whispered, "What's your name?"

She whispered, "My name is Lucy and I'm from Colombia."

Drick replied, "Nice to meet you. I am going to France for a day trip, do you want to come with me?"

Lucy answered, "Sorry, I have a husband and two children."

He continued. "We can go as friends, because I'm not trying to get married to you."

He whispered, "I have a wife and kid at home, too, that's not a problem: no one will know." He began to laugh and tried to shake her hand, but she pulled it away.

Drick pleaded, "Let's be great friends."

She responded to him nicely. "Look, you have your wife and I have my husband. Let's not make any more problems in our lives. Thank you very much for the offer, but no thanks."

Their conversation was interrupted by two beggars begging for money, but couldn't speak any English and had a note written on a piece of cardboard saying, "I am Albanian, please help me". Drick began searching in his pockets for some change to give them some money: he found £5 worth of change but being an extremely mean man he gave them £1. The lady looked at him in disbelief and angrily said, "Thank you," then they moved on.

Drick looked around for the young lady who was sitting near him, but she was not there. He thought, 'Oops,' then he took the newspaper out of his bag and began to read the FTSE 100 Index in the *Financial Times* while he proceeded on his train journey to work.

CHAPTER 4

THE LONDON BOMBING

As Drick sat on the train thinking about the beautiful young Colombian lady Lucy, he missed dating. A Middle Eastern man in about his middle twenties suddenly jumped up and began singing an Arabic song loudly in the train carriage. People thought he was crazy and started moving away from him. He dropped to the floor and started crying loudly, "I'm not worthy of living!" He started shouting, "I need to go, I need to go!"

He reached into his pocket and pulled out a set of pills. The man began popping them out of their cases into his hands, then asked if someone could give him something to drink. So a kind young man politely give him a new bottle of water which he took in his left hand. After opening his right hand, to everyone's astonishment there were about 15 pills in them.

At that instant he repeated, "I need to go, I need to go," and tried to swallow them, but a young lady noticed what the young man was about to do and slapped his hands away, splattering all the pills over the floor of the train. All the passengers on the train were hushed for a second because of what they had just witnessed.

Suddenly, there was an extremely loud bang on the train, as

they instantly screeched to a halt. Drick thought, 'My diabetes has exploded the blood vessels in my eyes,' because he couldn't see anything.

"Oh no!" he shouted. "I'm blind, I'm blind," then someone else screamed, "I'm blind, too!"

At that time various mutterings were coming from the passengers. It was clear that they all could not see because the place was dark. 'That is why,' Drick thought. 'I am okay: everyone else cannot see. In that case something is definitely causing us to have no light.'

One gentleman turned on the light from his phone, and to his horror there were bodies of people in the carriage. Due to this, many of the people began to turn on their phone lights; recognising the situation, people started screaming. Various people were crying for their loved ones. Several people were screaming because they couldn't find their legs.

One man cried out, "Where is my arm?" A woman threw something across the carriage and said, "I think that's your arm, mate." Drick thought, 'What a thing to do with someone's arm.' As more and more phone lights began to come on, the extent of what had happened was now being recognised. This was to some extent an extremely large explosion because everything was twisted.

Hence, feeling for his bodyparts to see if all of them were there, he subsequently stood up, and at that point shone the light from his phone on some rubble that was near his feet. It was his bag, stripped to pieces: all his medications and sandwiches were in bits.

'I need to get out of here,' he thought. At that point he tripped over a body. To his horror it was the body of the young man who had given up his brand new bottle of water to the Arabic man attempting suicide. Standing a few feet away looking dazed was the Arabic man who tried to commit suicide with the pills earlier on the train. He was still muttering his Arabic song. Drick thought how life was so disheartening: the person who wanted to die is still alive, and the person who wanted to live is now dead. He thought to himself, 'I need to get out of here,' but he kept tripping over dead bodies.

The incident was too much for Drick. He was very traumatised, and had dust all over his body, and began to feel dizzy. He quickly took out his diabetic injection pen, but recalling he had only injected himself an hour ago, Drick returned the pen to his pocket. Looking up and noticing there were twisted pieces of metal everywhere, at that moment he sat down on a piece of metal and fell asleep.

Drick felt a tapping on his shoulder. Opening his eyes, he recognised it was a fireman. "What's your name, sir?" he asked. "My name is Drick E Crawford and don't forget that."

The fireman said, "Let me help you out of here."

Drick asked the fireman, "Where are we?"

The fireman replied, "We are at Edgware station, sir."

Drick thought how lucky he was to be alive but was still millions of pounds in debt. While reflecting, Mr. Crawford thought of his mum, wife and kid. 'But the Russian mafia Radovan Bloodmic will stop at nothing to get his money: maybe I can disappear for a few months.'

A fireman tapped Mr. Crawford on his shoulder and uttered, "Let us get out of this station."

CHAPTER 5

PLANNING TO DISAPPEAR

As Drick came out of the Edgware station helped by a fireman, he looked to the left then to the right: there were police, firemen and ambulances everywhere. As he crossed the street a young lady held his hands and uttered, "Mr. Crawford." At first Drick didn't recognise her because she was covered in dust from the blast. It was Lucy, the Colombian lady he tried to date earlier in the train.

"Can I help you?"

"Yes," he answered. After recognising her, he muttered, "After this predicament can we go on a date?"

Lucy replied, "No, and now is not the time to be speaking about dating! I still have my husband and children, so I'm not interested. Did you forget that you told me about your wife and kid?"

Then she said goodbye and vanished into the crowd. Drick looked left and right: there were dozens of grey people, and no one looked black or white. Everyone was grey from the rubble of the blast. Drick asked where he could get a bus, but was told no buses were running because there was another explosion on one of the number 30 buses; furthermore, no buses were in operation.

A fireman came to him and said, "Excuse me, sir, could you

come with me?"

"For what?" questioned Drick.

The fireman pointed to Drick's arm that was covered in blood. Drick looked down at his arm and realised that he was cut. But he never felt anything. Regardless, he had to go to the hospital to have his cut stitched.

"Sit in that ambulance there," the fireman pointed. "It will take you to the hospital. Those two ambulances are taking walking wounded to the hospitals."

Hence, Drick sat in one of the ambulances then they left for the hospital. He tried to call his wife and his mother, but his phone battery had died. When the ambulance arrived at the hospital, the walking wounded were taken to special wards, depending on their level of injuries.

As Drick sat down he had time to think about everything that happened in his life for the last week. Drick thought, 'This would be the best time for me to disappear: no one would know what happened to me.' He remembered he had an old friend in Brighton named John. 'Maybe that will be the best place to go where no one knows me.' Drick began pondering: he could start a new life, free from the police and debt collector who would love to cut him into tiny pieces and mail his bodyparts home. 'But before that, I think I'll take a trip to New York this very moment.'

As he got to the ward he asked a nurse for a charger to charge his phone. At that moment he made a phone call, thus booking a flight from Gatwick to JFK Airport, then threw his phone away. He had made an arrangement when he arrived there: he would be met by his cousin Gully. While pondering, he thought about his family and how this would hurt his mum badly, but if he was killed by the Russian that would be worse.

Drick left the hospital, and went into a store and bought a new set of clothing. Afterwards he caught a cab to Gatwick, London, and flew by Virgin Atlantic to New York.

While travelling on the plane, he had six hours to think about what to do with his life. As Drick arrived at JFK Airport he was picked up by his cousin Gully. He explained to her his plans to disappear and not to tell anyone, not even his wife.

"Why?" Gully asked.

Drick responded. "Because everyone is after my money, Gully. I have the Russian mafia who were originally after me for three million but now is after me for five million. I have the Scotland Yard fraud detective after me for another couple of million. I even have the corner shop's owners after me for 25 pounds. I don't know what's happening with my life, Gully. I need to start a new life. Can you get me one of your friends for me to marry? I will pay them for their services."

Gully replied, "Not my friends, they aren't into that type of business, but I will try and help because you are my cousin."

A week went by before Gully called and stated that they would meeting up in an hour. She had found someone to do the business of marrying him. Drick was very happy. He thought, 'I could start a new life.'

A week went by, and he and his cousin met up with his cousin's friend Sharon, to arrange the marriage.

Drick's cousin had paid Sharon some money, so she could agree to get married. However, she did not tell Gully that she was two months pregnant and her baby's father was in prison, and due to come out in days. Subsequently they arranged to do a registry wedding the next day. Drick and his Gully got dressed and went to the registry the next day to meet Sharon. She got there early, and was looking very beautiful as they sat in the waiting room. Moments later, a gentleman about 6 feet 7 inches tall rushed into the registry, and spoke in a loud voice, "What the hell do you think you are doing?"

"Oh no!" Sharon screamed. "That's my baby father number three."

Drick thought, 'Baby father number three: what have I got myself into? I'm getting the hell out of here before I get killed. I have many people looking for me, and this now includes Sharon's crazy baby father who's going to kill me.' Instantly he grabbed his cousin, and they ran out of the registry as fast as they could.

"I am sorry," his cousin apologised. "I didn't know that she and her baby father were still together. She told me that they had broken up years ago: she lied."

"I will be getting my money back," said Gully. "I heard her baby father makes a living by killing policemen. That man is crazy: he will try to kill us now!" explained Gully. "Let's get the hell out of here."

So they jumped into the car and drove off.

The next day, Drick's cousin came to the house to collect him. Drick uttered, "Where are we going?"

Gully shouted angrily, "We're going to get our money back from that lady Sharon, she lied to me!"

Drick replied, "Don't worry about that money, Gully. I can give you the $3,000, that's not a problem."

"The money is not a problem," Gully declared, "it's the principle."

Drick thought, 'I didn't get killed for millions of pounds, but now I'm going to get killed for $3,000.'

"I am not concerned. I gave her my $3,000," declared Gully, "and we are going to get it back."

"Are we going alone?" Drick asked.

"No, we are not going alone," answered Gully.

"I'm going to pick up my boyfriend, Dexter."

'Great,' Drick thought, 'how much worse can this day become? Dexter is a Drug Enforcement Administration (DEA) agent, and he always carries two guns with him. This is getting crazier by the second. I'm going to die for $3,000 in America, when I owed other people millions of pounds in London and would still be alive. What a way to die, what a cheap way to die.'

They drove to Dexter's house and picked him up: as he entered the car Drick noticed the bulge in his waist and the bulge by his ankle. Dexter was carrying his two guns; they drove across to meet Sharon in Brooklyn. While driving to Sharon's house, Drick was whispering his prayers, because he thought today would be his last day alive: he knew that Dexter had two guns and he did not know how many guns Sharon's baby father had. He expected to be in a war zone any minute now only for $3,000.

When they got there, to Drick's surprise there were about five police cars: her third baby father had beaten up her fourth baby father and was physically arrested and led away by the police.

"There she is," pointed Gully.

Drick's cousin strode up to Sharon, and demanded, "Where is my money?" To his surprise, Sharon opened her bag and give the $3,000 back to Gully. "Thank you very much," replied his cousin. "I thought this was going to be a big problem."

"No," replied Sharon, "I've got enough problems." Drick was a thrilled man, because the big shoot-out he was expecting did not happen, so they hastily left the area.

Drick spent two more weeks trying to get another woman to get married. He didn't like the choice of women his cousin got him. But he was not successful, so he came back to London, and was going to attempt to live in Brighton with his friend John and his girlfriend. Meanwhile, his mum and family were grieving for Drick, because he was presumed dead.

CHAPTER 6

DRICK REPORTED MISSING

Drick's mum Augusta was watching the 6 pm news on TV in her kitchen when she heard the broadcasters speaking about the London bombing that happened a few weeks ago and they are still hunting for the bombers. She sat there thinking what had happened to her son. She was told by the police when she was at the station that after six weeks an official missing persons report can be filed. Augusta remembered this was one of Drick's routes to work, because he travelled through Edgware station. It had been a few weeks since the bombing, and they hadn't heard from Drick. Augusta picked up her phone and tried calling Drick again; she has been doing this for a few weeks. But there was no answer, so she thought, 'I will call his wife Seri and find out if she spoke to him recently.'

Augusta called his wife and said, "I was trying to call him for weeks but got no answer."

"Mum, I am worried," exclaimed Seri. "It has been weeks since he did not call. I know he is not fine: you know he always calls us to let us know what's happened to him," Seri uttered to his mum.

While trying to hide her fear, she added, "Mum, I didn't mean to worry you."

His mum replied, "But that is my only child."

Seri thought, 'Something definitely is wrong. I haven't heard from Drick, and it has been weeks since he left home for work. His mother uttered that she rang him about 15 times and got no reply.' She stated, "My son doesn't do that, he usually would call after the third time when I call him. He always would return my calls and say what's up."

She kept calling Seri twice every hour throughout the night, and early in the morning. At about 10 am Seri switched off her phone because every time Mum called, she was crying. Seri tried to call some of Drick's friends the next day but they had not seen him; after that she called the workplace and asked if he had reported for work, but he had not. So she called a cab in the evening and started to search for him again in the hospitals. She had been doing this for weeks. Later that evening, Seri called Drick's mother and said, "I have searched for weeks, and checked every hospital and did not find him."

Drick's mum replied, "I did the same, and I even checked police stations to see if he was locked up." Seri was now crying aloud on the phone. Mum responded. "I will be coming over to your house immediately," so she hung up the phone and called a cab to take her to Seri's house.

When she got there, Mum and Seri began hugging and crying together, because Drick was now feared dead. Seri said to his mum, "We will have to go to the police station and report him as being missing."

She continued. "I don't feel like my son died."

Seri replied, "But he has not come home for weeks."

So both of them and James went to the police station to report Drick as missing. When they got there, the sergeant at the desk took all of Drick's details and stated, because of this situation, "It may take weeks before we get back to you."

Mum muttered to the sergeant, "I feel it in my spirit that my son is not dead, but I cannot prove it."

The Sergeant said, "I know how you feel: it's some mothers' instinct, and they are always correct. I have spoken to many mums over the past few weeks and they said the same thing."

The sergeant filled the report. Afterwards, Seri, Mum and James left the police station and went home.

A few weeks went by. Mum began going to church frequently in the week, and on Sunday she would go twice: she was praying that one day she would see her son Drick. Mum was telling everyone about her son being missing when one of Mum's church friends explained that her grandson was an expert on computers, and she could ask him to put Drick's picture on the computer, so all of the parishioners in the Catholic church could see.

"It's an excellent idea," declared Mum, "let's do it." So Mum took one of Drick's photos from her bag and gave it to her friend's grandson. The gentleman submitted Drick's photograph onto the internet.

A week went by, and then one of the church parishioners saw Drick's picture on the internet: they were living in Cardiff, Wales. They claimed they saw a man looking just like Drick sleeping rough in the Morrisons car park.

Drick's mum got very excited and called his wife Seri, and told her what the lady had revealed about seeing Drick sleeping rough in a Morrisons car park.

The next day they caught the train to Cardiff Central station, then they got into a cab and went to the Morrisons car park.

Seri remarked, "If my husband is sleeping rough I need to buy him some new clothing." Then she went into a clothing store. Mum could not contain her emotion; she rushed to where a gentleman was sleeping and shouted, "Drick, my son!" The man turned and answered, "Yes that's me." Then Mum grabbed the man's hands, and took him into the nearby cafe and bought him a cup of coffee. Seri came out of the store and found that Mum had disappeared. She called Mum on her mobile phone and said, "Where are you?"

Mum responded. "I am sitting in the cafe with Drick."

Seri replied, "Okay, I will come there and find you."

Seri found the cafe and walked in, but she could not see Mum, so she called her phone again, hence Mum stood up and waved, "I'm over here."

Seri walked over to the table where Mum and a gentleman sat. "Here is my son, we found him," announced Mum excitedly.

The gentleman was sitting there looking very bemused. Seri looked at the gentleman and declared, "That's not Drick, Mum."

"This is not my husband," then she asked him to remove his shirt to see if his right shoulder had a tattoo, but to their surprise there was none.

"This is not your son, Mum."

Mum muttered, "He responded to me when I called him."

The man said, "You called my name: Derrick."

Mum confessed, "Derrick, I'm sorry."

Then she started crying. Seri and Derrick consoled her, hence they got into a cab and went back to Cardiff Central station, and soon after they began their journey back to London.

Weeks went by when they got another call from a parishioner in Aberdeen, Scotland, who stated they knew Drick and he was living with his wife in Scotland.

Mum called Seri and told her: she was annoyed about hearing Drick having a new wife and declared she would not be going to Scotland. Hence, Mum went by herself and got a cab from the station to the address she was given. Mum got to the address and rang the doorbell. A lady opened the door and said, "Hello, I'm Mrs. Crawford and how can I help you, madam?"

Mum explained that she was the lady who rang about Drick her son.

The wife replied, "I never knew Drick's mum was still alive."

"I'm certainly alive," said Augusta. She asked where Drick was: his wife pointed to the garden. Mum was ecstatic and ran into the garden, but she didn't notice a gentleman sitting on a small bench doing some gardening, when Mum accidentally crashed into him, knocking him over.

The gentleman got up, laughing, and said, "Hello, I am Drick, how can I help you, Mum?"

Mum became sad immediately, because she noticed this was not her son Drick. A shirtless gentleman explained his name as Drick E Crawford. At that moment Mum noticed he had a tattoo on his right shoulder. But it was of a horse, not of a heart. Mum dropped to her knees and started crying. "Oh no, I will never find my son alive again."

Drick E Crawford consoled Mum. Drick laughingly declared, "I can be your son if you want, because I don't have a mother." Hence he made Mum, his wife and himself a few cups of coffee. Afterwards they drove Mum back to the train station. She said goodbye, then caught the train back to London. Mum thought, 'I will never see my son alive again but I will never give up, because I feel he's still alive.'

In the meantime, Drick was alive and was trying to live in America, and was not successful. He had to return and was now planning to go and start a new life in Brighton.

CHAPTER 7

SLEEPING ROUGH

Drick was on his way back from America where he was for a few weeks. He thought he couldn't live in London anymore. 'I will be moving to Brighton where I have a friend named John. Maybe my life will get better. He said if I have any problems I must call him: he will be more than welcome for me to stay in his five-bedroom house. I helped him out years ago when he was just starting his business: he owes me a favour.'

Drick called John and said, "John, it is me, Drick. Remember you said if I need a favour I must call you. I do need that favour now please."

John replied, "No problem: come to Brighton anytime."

Then Drick quickly explained that he needed to come right away.

John clarified, "That's not a problem."

Thus Drick caught a National Express coach from Victoria and went to Brighton. But he didn't have much money left, due to the fact that all of his bank assets had been frozen.

Drick got to Brighton and thought, 'This would be nice to get away from that Radovan and Earl because they are always hunting me. No one will know where I am living now.'

As Drick got to the coach station in Brighton, he was picked up by John and his girlfriend. She looked at him and smiled in a scrutinising way. Drick took no notice of her because all he wanted was a place to sleep, and to reset his life.

A week went by, and Drick was happy when one day he noticed John's girlfriend wearing some very tight clothing when she was at home alone with him. Drick tried to keep his eyes off her, but she would find ways of bumping into him. He took no notice of her: this went on for weeks, and Drick tried his best to stay away from her. Then one day he observed she was wearing a bathroom robe, while she deliberately walked into him and dropped her bathroom robe: to Drick's amazement she had no clothing on. Then she began walking around the house naked. Drick quickly grabbed the robe and ran after her, but she ran away. Drick thought, 'I am not going to be playing this game.'

So he quickly got his towel and got into the bathroom; moments later he heard a banging on the bathroom door. "Let me in!" she shouted. "I want to use the toilet right away."

Drick blurted out, "Couldn't you use the other toilets?" because he knew there were two other toilets and bathrooms in the house.

She shouted, "I don't like those toilets, I like this one and this is my house, so let me in."

Drick thought, 'This is going to be trouble, because her boyfriend owns the house, and I have no other alternative but to let her into the bathroom.'

He opened the bathroom door and let her into the bathroom.

She rushed into the bathroom but did not want to use the toilet. Instead she grabbed Drick's towel and threw it under the shower; the towel became wet instantly. Drick quickly got out of the shower and tried to run swiftly to his room, to get a dry towel. John's girlfriend came running naked from her bedroom, and began chasing Drick around the house, while laughing loudly.

At that moment the front door suddenly opened. It was John, who accidentally came home early from work. For that second everyone froze. John screamed at Drick, "What are you doing with my girlfriend?!"

Drick muttered, "Nothing: your girlfriend threw my towel under the shower and it got wet, so I'm hurrying to get a dry towel from my room, that's the only thing I'm doing."

John shouted at her, "Why are you naked?!"

She didn't say anything but just went into their bedroom. John followed her into their bedroom. His girlfriend blurted, "Honey, you know I like to be in the house naked, now you have brought your friend here. Get him out, or I am leaving."

John came out of the bedroom and looked at Drick angrily and said, "You're leaving my house, you've got 10 minutes."

Drick looked at John and started crying, then declared, "I did not do anything with your girlfriend, she was trying to come on to me, but thanks, John, I will be leaving in nine minutes I don't need all 10 of your minutes."

Drick began collecting his clothing hurriedly and left the house crying because he didn't know where he was going to be living that night. He had no other friends in Brighton. Lucky it was summer:

Drick walked with his bags to a nearby park, then sat on one of the benches.

He observed there were a few people sitting on the other benches drinking cans of beers, laughing and smelling funky. Drick thought, 'I am a diabetic but I am feeling very thirsty. If only I can have a can of beer. I have had nothing to eat or drink for the day. I am never going to be one of those guys.' Suddenly one of the guys got up and came over and offered him a brand new can of beer to drink.

Drick said, "Thank you very much," because he didn't know when the next time he would be eating, and how long he would be living on the streets. The gentleman who gave Drick the beer sat down beside him and said, "My name is David, what's yours?"

Drick replied, "My name is Drick, nice to meet you," and they shook hands.

David said, "You are new around here, and these are my drinking friends."

"Yes, I'm new around here," responded Drick. "I've been in this park for two hours."

David laughed and said, "Two hours."

"Yes!" replied Drick. "Two hours. Three hours was living with the friend when his girlfriend created some big disturbance between me and my friend, after that she got me kicked out instantly."

David said, "You don't worry. I know some warm places we can sleep when it becomes dark. There is an old lady at the end of the road that lets me into her house to have a bath and number two."

"Okay," acknowledged Drick. "That's the reason why you don't look like you are sleeping on the streets."

"It's a hard life out here," continued David. "People treat you extremely badly, so I try my best to be as clean as possible. It's getting dark," David remarked, "let's go home."

Drick laughed and replied, "We have no home."

David got up and beckoned Drick. "Follow me. We will pass by Auntie Patsy's and have a bath first, and then we'll go home."

"Okay," replied Drick, "let's go."

So they got off the bench and went to David's auntie's house. David took out his mobile phone and called her. Auntie Patsy opened the door. She looked about 60 years old. David said, "Auntie Patsy, meet my good friend, Drick, it is his first day sleeping rough. We would like to have a bath and go."

Auntie answered, "No problem, you know where the bath is, David."

Then she made some sandwiches for them: they both had a shower and said bye to Auntie Patsy, and left the house. Drick asked, "Where is home?"

"Our home is over there, where those containers are: the first one to the left is mine, and my friends live in the others."

To Drick's surprise, David pulled out a set of keys and opened one of the padlocks on the container. They entered the container: to Drick's astonishment there was a bed, a portable light, and a small wardrobe system where you could put your clothing.

Drick remarked, "This is a nice place you have here."

"Thank you," muttered David. "I found all of this stuff on the streets, and put them together to make myself comfortable."

"I got help from some of the boys in the yard, and there is a geek who is living nearby who helped me hugely with the lighting system. I tried my best with a water system, but we have to fetch water around here."

"Okay," Drick declared, "that's not a problem: this is better than me sleeping out on the park bench tonight."

Afterwards, they talked about life for about a couple of hours. David said, "What type of work did you use to do before you became homeless?"

"I was a music video producer," replied Drick.

David remarked, "I used to play bass guitars in different bands. That's the reason why we became friends quickly: the reason is both of us are into the music business."

Drick did not know when he fell asleep: he was awoken suddenly by a loud bang. David awoke and asked Drick if he was okay.

David explained to Drick that some kids in the nearby estate loved to throw big bricks at the containers.

Then David went back to sleep, but Drick could not get to sleep. He thought of his wife, kid, friends and mum, because she would definitely form a search party to find him, then she would report him missing.

CHAPTER 8

A NEW WIFE AND KID

Drick awoke the next day and asked David, "Are you still in contact with anyone from the music industry?"

"Yes!" replied David. "I'm meeting Crispin Jacobs, who plays bass in the Band Crazy-World."

Drick burst out, "His brother Pat Jacobs and I went to the same university in London. We studied Video Music Technology." Drick had a very large smile on his face.

David muttered, "What are you smiling for?"

Drick responded. "That's my friend, I haven't seen him in years. Oh, what a small world we are living in. Can I come with you to meet him?"

"Sure," replied David. "I am meeting him today at 1 pm."

Later that day they got dressed and went to meet Crispin. As they walked into the studio Crispin recognised Drick: he was really ecstatic to see him. Crispin came over and hugged him instantly, then thanked David for bringing Drick to meet him.

Crispin said, "David, I asked you to come here because I have a job for you playing bass on some musical tracks I'm making for a TV series."

David responded: "Thank you very much."

Drick uttered, "I am looking for work, too."

"No problem," continued Crispin. "You can help me direct the series: it starts in a week. I have to leave now."

Drick started work the following week. When he collected his first paycheck he bought himself an old car and rented a room. Weeks went by when Drick got a phone call from his friend Crispin saying there is going to be a musicians' party, at one of the studios on Saturday and there are going to be lots of pretty women there. Drick thought, 'This is the best time to get an adorable girlfriend.'

When Saturday evening came, he got dressed and went to the party. As he stepped into the hall it seemed like all of the musicians knew him: they were shaking his hand and making fun of him.

Somebody asked him, "How is life?"

He lied and stated it was excellent. "I'm here to find a lady."

Whilst the night went on, Drick noticed many pretty women were dancing in very short skirts and trousers. Drick became thirsty: hence he began walking towards the bar when he bumped into a lady and spilled her drink from a glass over her trousers.

"Oops sorry!" said Drick. "Can I buy you another drink?"

She smiled and muttered, "Thank you very much, you can."

Drick responded. "Lead the way to the bar, please."

He noticed she was beautiful in the front and behind: as they continued towards the bar her hips were swaying up and down. The lady saw Drick looking at her bum, and asked, "Do you like the view?"

"Yeah, I do," he replied. "Does that body belong to anyone?" as he pointed to her bum.

She answered, "It depends on what you mean by belonging to anyone."

Drick replied, "I mean do you have a gentleman in your life?"

The lady replied, "No! Do you want to be that gentleman?" she asked.

"Certainly," Drick said in response. "I would love to be in control of a body like that."

They got to the bar and pulled up two stools, just as Drick asked, "What drink did I spill over you?"

The lady replied, "Rum and Coke."

Drick continued. "I am new to this area. I need someone to show me around this town. Sorry for being rude, my name is Drick."

The lady said in response, "My name is Diane, I can show you around: here is my number."

Drick took a business card out of his pocket and said, "Here is my name and number. Now may I have a dance, please, Miss Diane?"

They both left the bar and went to the dance floor, but then Drick noticed she was pulling him closer and breathing on his neck. He thought, 'This is my type of woman.'

After they finished dancing, he arranged to take her for lunch the next day.

The next day they met, and went to a restaurant to have lunch. Diane explained to Drick that she had one child and was single. Drick asked if she was working.

She replied, "No I'm in between jobs."

Then Drick asked, "Can we go to lunch next week, Monday?"

She answered, "That's okay."

A week went by, and they met at the restaurant as arranged. Drick questioned, "How did you get here?"

She responded, "I got here by public transport."

He boasted, "I have a car," and offered to take her home.

Once they got to her house she said, "Park your car and come inside."

Drick replied, "Thanks, I will be there soon."

He parked the car then entered the house. As he sat in the chair, he noticed there was not just one picture, but five kids' pictures on the walls.

"Is this your family?" he asked.

She answered, "Yes."

Drick continued. "I thought you said you only had one child."

She uttered, "Oops, I forgot about the other four because they don't live with me, they live with their father."

Drick thought, 'How many other kids does she have?'

She asked, "Are you afraid of kids? Don't worry, they don't live with me all the time."

She grabbed Drick and threw him to the floor. Drick jumped up and questioned:

"What are you doing?"

"I'm going to make passionate love to you," Diane responded.

Drick responded, "Sorry, Diane, I don't do unprotected sex!"

She whispered, "That's not a problem, I have some condoms here."

Diane placed a condom on Drick's private part and began

making love roughly to him. Drick thought, 'This is great and she knows what she's doing.'

When they were finished Diane got up and went to the bathroom. He rose from the floor, and his hands accidentally knocked off a few condoms that were on the table.

Bending over to pick up the condoms, he noticed when he squeezed them that there was air coming out of the condom packets. He began to press the other condoms. Someone had deliberately put holes in them. He called out to Diane and showed her the three condom packets. He asked, "What's this?"

"What's what?" she questioned.

Drick uttered, "These are punctured condom packets: are you trying to trap me?"

"No!" Diane muttered. "I'm on contraceptives, don't worry."

Drick shouted, "Oops, I forgot I had a meeting," and hurried out of the house.

Weeks went by when suddenly Diane's phone calls became frequent. Drick was not answering her, because he was annoyed. Drick finally answered the phone and asked Diane what was happening. She said that she was pregnant, thus claiming she got pregnant because there was a mix-up with her contraceptive dates.

Then she questioned him: what was he going to do about her having his baby?

Drick replied, "I told you those condoms were punctured and you were trying to trap me."

Diane began crying, then she burst out, "All the men I have children with don't love me!"

Drick thought that was why she wasn't married to them, then he told her not to cry. He responded. "I will always love you, and I would love it if you could have my baby."

She replied, "We will have to be married." She didn't like having children without being married.

Drick muttered, "Okay," without even thinking. Because he knew he couldn't go back to see his first child. He knew this was his best chance to see his child grow up before his eyes, and he would be walking the street with someone as beautiful as Diane.

Weeks later, they got married in the registry office because Drick said he didn't want a large wedding. The relationship was moving at a breakneck pace; furthermore, it was only three months after they had first met. Life was great for the next three months.

Then one day Diane came into the house and told Drick that she would like to speak to him about a vital matter.

"Okay," said Drick, "let's talk about this matter in the dining room." Diane explained her kid's father has lost his job, and the four kids would be coming to live with them.

"What?!" Drick shouted. "Are you insane? How can I look after six children, when only one of them belongs to me?"

Diane started crying, and uttered, "What is mine is yours, and if you love me you will take care of all my children. I can't have them sleeping on the streets."

Drick responded. "Okay, when are they coming?"

Diane muttered, "In an hour!"

"An hour!?" Drick screamed. "How long ago did you know about this?"

"A week ago," she answered.

Drick continued. "You are telling me an hour before they arrive. Do you know you're crazy, woman?"

"Sorry," she replied, "but someone told him I had married a rich man, and we could afford to look after all six of the children. Hence, he sent them over after he lost his job."

Drick looked at her angrily and commented, "My name is Drick E Crawford and don't forget that!"

Then he went into the bedroom and put some clothing in a small bag and left the house.

The next day he had to return home for his suit because he was having a meeting with some musicians. She spouted, "Where were you last night?"

Drick murmured, "With a friend."

"Okay," she continued. "I am going to the shop. I will be back in 15 minutes: stay with the children please."

"Okay," declared Drick, "I will."

Diane left the house and went shopping, but returned home hours after. She was smiling and spouted, "Well, I ran into some friends."

Drick asked, "Did you forget I said I was having a meeting this morning?"

"No, I didn't," responded Diane. "You can have the meeting tomorrow."

This made Drick very angry.

Afterwards every week on Mondays and Thursdays, Diane would say, "I am going shopping," and wouldn't return home until hours later.

One Thursday Drick got extremely angry and left the children by themselves in the house, and followed his wife to where she claimed she was shopping. To his astonishment she was meeting with a gentleman, and they were laughing, punching each other gleefully. Drick jumped out of his car and walked towards where Diane and the man were standing.

He asked, "Who is this?"

She replied, "This is my kids' father: we're trying to sort out our child support problems."

Drick blurted out, "That's a delightful way to sort out your child support problems. Is that done by playing with each other?"

He got into the car and drove off speedily. Diane continued meeting her kids' father for months on every Monday and Thursday in the mall in Brighton. One day one of the children got angry at Drick and told him off.

He replied, "You cannot speak to me like that because I'm not your father."

Drick got very angry. "I'm going to the shop to buy sweeties." When Diane returned from her shopping trip she found the children home alone. When she asked where Drick was, the children told her he went to the shop to buy sweeties four hours ago, but never came back.

Weeks went by, but Drick never returned: he had rented a new room and started a new life again.

CHAPTER 9

MEETING AT THE DENTIST

One Thursday morning, Seri, Drick's ex-wife, woke and said she would like to visit her sister in Brighton. Hence, she and her new husband packed the car and drove to Brighton. When they got to Brighton, Her son James said that his tooth was hurting. On account of this they called the nearest dentist and made an appointment: they were told that the appointment was 2 pm later that day.

An hour later Seri was getting her son James ready for his appointment, when she suddenly began crying.

Her husband Paul said, "What are you crying for?"

She muttered, "I miss my ex-husband, Drick."

Paul responded angrily, "How long do we have to carry on like this? Every time you think of your ex-husband you start crying."

Seri responded. "I miss him because he usually would take his son to the dentist. I would be able to get to sleep as long as I pleased, but now I will have to take him myself to the dentist. Do you know how hard it is to make a child go to the dentist when he doesn't want to go?"

Paul answered, "Okay, I will take him, no problem."

Seri exclaimed, "Oh no, not my son! He's my son, and I will take him myself."

Paul replied, "Let's not argue. If you're going to take him I will drive you there."

They got into the car and drove a few minutes to the dentist. The only person's voice that could be heard was James saying his tooth hurt.

Seri said, "Can you wait here for me, Paul? I wouldn't be long." Then she and James exited the car and went to the dentist's reception.

Seri said to the receptionist, "Hello, my name is Seri: this is my son James Crawford to see the dentist please."

The receptionist said, "This is a very special day: we have two James Crawfords in the dentistry today. You may have a seat please."

Seri thought, 'It would be nice to see the child who has the same name as my son. I wonder what he looks like.' Then she sat down quietly and began playing with James. A little boy about three years old wandered over and started playing with James. A few minutes later his mother came over and said, "Leave this boy to play, come here have a seat."

He started crying for a few seconds then stopped because his mum gave him a sweet.

A voice came over the loudspeaker saying, "James Crawford to dentist number one door, please."

Seri and the mother of the boy who was playing with James got up and went to the same dentist number one's door.

They looked at each other. As they stepped towards the dentist's door, Seri said, "My name is Seri, and this is my son, James Crawford."

The lady said, "My name is Diane and this is my son, James Crawford. There must have been some mistake here." So they went back to the reception.

The receptionist said, "Diane was here before you, so she can go in first to see the dentist, then you can go after."

"Okay," said Seri then sat back down.

About 15 minutes later, Diane came out with her son and motioned to Seri: you could go in now.

"I will wait for you, and it's some sort of coincidence that both of our sons have the same name."

Subsequently she waited for Seri, then Seri came out of the dentist's room 15 minutes later. They sat down and began to speak.

Seri said her son's father's name was Drick E Crawford.

Diane looked amazed and said, "This is a big coincidence because my ex-husband's name was Drick E Crawford and he used to be a music producer, but he suddenly disappeared."

Seri replied, "My husband's name was Drick E Crawford as well: he died in the London bombing, and they never found his body again. I miss him so much, even though he was a bit of an arrogant man, and he always walked around saying, 'My name is Drick E Crawford and don't forget that'."

Seri responded, "Oh my God, my husband said the same thing: 'My name is Drick E Crawford and don't forget that'. What a coincidence: maybe they were twins: my husband had a tattoo of a heart with 'Mum' written in the centre. He said he had that tattoo to remind him about the love his mum has for him and the struggles she went through to make him a man: the tattoo was on his right shoulder. Also, he spoke of some accountant that took all of his money. The accountant used to work for Sting, the musician."

Diane continued. "My ex-husband also said his accountant used to work for Sting. That's an extreme coincidence. When did your husband die?"

Seri responded. "My husband died in the London bombing in July 2005."

"That's strange," stated Diane. "I got married November 2005. Seven months afterwards, I had James, will then said he still was living when he left me in 2007 so he couldn't have died in 2005, that's impossible."

"I think we're speaking about the same man here, Seri. I can feel it in my soul."

"We're talking about the same man because he always seemed to be nervous when calling James's name. Now I understand why because he knew he had another son named James." Seri continued. "I have an address his mum give to me. She got it from one of his friends who thought Drick might be living in Leeds. I at first I thought Mum was crazy, but Mum was correct: her son was still alive and living in Leeds. Mum always felt that her son never died on that day. This is even crazier, because she was right all these years, but now I am going to check that address out. Do you want to come with me and see if we can find him?"

"Yes, I will!" replied Diane. "I would like to see his face when he recognises that both of us know what tricks he was up to. While he was living with me for a couple of years."

Diane continued. "Then in the last three months of our relationship, he always seemed to be very nervous and was always looking out of the window frequently. When I asked him what was up, he would respond, 'Nothing.' I recognise that for three weeks there were two Mercedes Jeeps parked outside the house. I also noticed when his mobile phone rang, he would leave the house and go into the garage to speak."

Seri took Diane's number and said, "I have to go because someone is waiting for me."

Then she said goodbye to Diane, and ran out of the dentist's and jumped into her car. She started crying, furiously saying, "That bastard Drick is still alive!"

Her new husband Paul said, "What?! I thought he was dead. It would be amazing to see what you two ladies would do to him if you find out he is living here in Brighton."

CHAPTER 10

THE CALLS

Paul, Seri's husband, was correct. Drick was living in Brighton about 15 streets away. He was living in a room which he rented. While in his room relaxing on the bed, he was wondering, 'My life is like a wave: it's always going up and down. What's next?' He got up and took his diabetic injection, also did his daily exercise, made breakfast and left for work. While driving to work he began feeling dizzy, so he drove into a McDonald's car park, then took out a small carrier case he kept in the back of his car: in it he had a diabetic blood tester. Then he tested his blood: to his surprise it was 20. But this is not good: it was way above the required 8, so he took out an injection pen from his pocket and injected himself.

Drick stepped into McDonald's to buy himself a meal when his phone started ringing. 'Who could it be ringing me so early in the morning?' he thought.

Drick answered the phone and a voice said, "Hello, this is your wife, Seri."

He thought this was one of his friends playing games with him so he said, "Seri?! I don't know any Seri."

The female voice said angrily, "Your first wife, the one that gave birth to your son James Crawford. I was grieving for you, I thought you were dead."

Drick replied, "I'm okay, just had a little problem. Sorry you thought I was dead."

Seri uttered, "You are a nasty man. You left your wife, you left your son, and you left your mother who is a very heartbroken woman. I thought your mother was crazy when she said she had a feeling that you were not dead. But I am the craziest one here because you were alive all these years."

Seri continued. "Drick, are you in some sort of trouble? Because two men have been calling me for years asking if I have seen or heard from you. One of them has a Russian accent, and the other is an inspector from Scotland Yard. They told me that as soon as I hear from you, I must call them immediately."

"Oh no, please don't call them," begged Drick.

"Sorry, too late, Drick," mentioned Seri, "I've called them already. The Russian guy said thank you very much, and he mailed me $3,000 because I called him. He seemed to be a very nice and polite man. He said he grew up with his mother only because his father left them when he was a baby, and he knows what it is to be an only child. He stated that you owe his company £5 million and he would like to have it now."

Seri continued. "I never knew we had that much money because you always didn't have any money when I asked you. I had to explain to him that you were killed in the London bombing. But he thought, like your mum, you weren't dead. Oh dear, your second wife Diane will be happy to know that I found you. I met her a few months ago at the dentist's. Why didn't you tell her you were married? You're a mentally insane man because you've named your second son James Crawford as well. How could you do such a thing to that woman? You left her with six children. She said she was perfectly married when you came and broke up her happy home, then you made her kids' father lose his job because he started to drink."

"That was a lie!" Drick replied. "She had four of her children living with their father separately when I met her. Only one child was living with her, and she said she forgot she had more children."

Seri continued. "I'm not sorry for you, because you also had your mum going all over the United Kingdom searching for you. She went to Wales looking for you, and then she went to Scotland looking for you. Augusta went everywhere looking for you; she also had every Catholic and non-Catholic church looking for you. Mum placed some of your pictures on the internet. What a heartless son you are. The Inspector from Scotland Yard was happy to know that you're alive."

He explained. "You are to answer charges for tax evasion, I also gave him your phone number because you had all of us thinking that you were dead."

"Why did you do that?" asked Drick.

Seri replied, "Because you're a very nasty man and I want you to feel the pain that you put us through. I will be seeing you one of these days if one of these people don't get you." Then she hung up.

Drick finished his meal and left the McDonald's. He got into his car and drove to work. He parked his car in the workplace car park. When his phone began ringing again, this made Drick very nervous.

"Hello, good day."

"Is this Mr. Drick E Crawford?" a voice asked.

"Yes!" responded Drick.

The voice replied, "My name is Radovan: remember me? Where is my money? It's been years, and you still haven't paid me. Now I have your number, I will be coming to collect my money soon. If your wives don't get you or the police don't get you, I will get you. I will see you soon." Then he hung up the phone.

Drick new the next caller would always be the Detective Inspector Earl Killhill: he always called minutes after Radovan hung up. So the phone began to ring, and Drick answered and said, "Hello Mr. Earl Killhill. I heard you'll be looking for me."

"Yes!" replied the inspector. "I heard you died and came back to life. Do you know I was becoming depressed when I heard you were dead? Afterwards, I heard the good news about you still being alive, and I was happy because I would be able to find you eventually. I now can continue hunting for you. See you soon, Mr. Drick E Crawford, and don't forget that." The inspector laughed and hung up the phone.

The phone was quiet for a second when it started to ring again, and he noticed that it was a different number, so he answered.

"Hello, this is Drick."

A voice said, "It's me, Diane. I've been looking for you everywhere, then your first wife gave me this number, so I am coming with my kids' father to collect James's child support. I need all my money right away, see you soon."

Then she hung up the phone. Drick muttered to himself, "This impossible. How can my four enemies call me five minutes apart? I'm getting out of town soon: this is too close for comfort." He thought, 'I need to be extremely careful. Because one of these days my wives and my enemy will be knocking on my door, so I am going to Leeds.'

CHAPTER 11

ON THE RUN

Drick was getting ready for a meeting at a studio when his doorbell rang. He looked out of the window and saw it was his first wife, Seri. He was extremely shocked, and thought, 'How did she know where I was living?' She looked up and saw Drick peering out of the window, and she shouted, "Get yourself down here now, and open this door! Your son would like to see you."

'It was good and bad,' he thought. It was bad because his first wife Seri had found him, and it was good because he had the chance to see his son James Crawford for the first time in years. As he opened the door, his wife rushed into the house. She slapped him, saying, "How could you do this to your son and me? What have we done to you? We thought you were dead all these years." At that moment she started crying.

She continued. "You had your mother and I thinking that you died in the London bombing. What type of man are you? You had your son also assuming that his dad had died years ago, while you disappeared and left me with a mortgage. The bank was trying to take the houses. I had to sell the studios, borrow money from your friends and your mum. I tried to keep the houses," Seri explained.

"I tried so hard to keep up with the mortgages. The bank eventually took the houses: are you not ashamed of yourself?"

Seri turned to her son and blurted out, "James says hi to his no good father."

James was his first son and 9 years old. The kid said, "He's not my father: my father died in the London bombing, and my daddy is outside in the car."

Seri declared, "This is what you have done: even your son thinks you're dead. You need to come downstairs to the car and meet my new husband who's a bodyguard, and you know they don't mess with people. He really would like to rip your head from your body because of the things you put his son through."

Drick was afraid but he came out to the car to meet her new husband. At that moment a very large gentleman emerged from the car. Seri shouted:

"Paul, meet Drick, my ex-husband!" To Drick's astonishment, the gentleman began running towards him. He turned and began running for his life. He thought while running, 'This guy Paul is a very mean-looking man, and I don't want him to catch me.'

At that time Drick saw two people trying to stop him: they jumped out of a parked car in front of him, but he managed to run around them. He had a glimpse of the woman, and he recognised her: she was his second wife, Diane, and her ex-husband. Drick thought, 'I need to run faster: I have two ex-wives and their husbands after me.' He found where his car was parked and quickly jumped into the vehicle, then speedily drove off. While looking into the rear-view mirror, he observed two vehicles driving erratically behind his car, trying to catch him. He drove for about three minutes, then turned left without recognising it was a car park. The two cars screeched to a halt: they had boxed Drick's car into a corner. Four people abruptly jumped out of the vehicles: he noticed they were two men and his two ex-wives. He also observed there were two children: Seri's son James, about 9 years old, and Diane's son James, the child who was about five years old.

Seri shouted, "Let me beat him up!" Just then she kicked off her shoes, and threw them at Drick.

As Seri's new husband grabbed Drick, she hurriedly picked up her shoes again and hit him over the head. This caused Drick to start bleeding. Meanwhile, Diane and her husband were kicking and stomping on Drick. The fight maybe lasted a few minutes, but to Drick it seemed to have been an hour. They suddenly stopped when two black Mercedes Jeeps pulled into the car park and screeched to a halt. They got scared and jumped into their cars and drove off, because they thought the Mercedes Jeeps had Drick's friends in them. One of the windows on the passenger side of the second Jeep opened and someone popped their head out and said, "Hello, Mr. Drick E Crawford," in a Russian accent, "I can see that you have more enemies than I thought." It was Radovan Bloodmic, the debt collector. Then he opened the Mercedes door and said to Drick, "Get in now."

Suddenly police sirens could be heard, and they were getting louder and louder. Radovan said to his driver, "Let's go," then he pointed to Drick in a gun-like motion and said, "I will be seeing you later." At that moment the two black Mercedes Jeeps frantically drove off from the car park speedily. Drick cleaned himself up and quickly put on a hat he had in the boot of the car, so that he could hide the wounds on his head from the police. At the same time the police cars screeched to a halt in their cars.

Four policemen jumped out and uttered, "Did someone call us? They said a man was being beaten up by two women and two men in this car park."

Drick uttered, "Yes, I saw the man: he was running away with blood pouring from his head. They jumped out of their cars punching and kicking him, so he ran that way."

The police said thank you and drove off.

Drick drove himself to the hospital to be checked out. He told the nurse he was running and fell over, whacking his head. As he drove himself home from the hospital he began to feel a sharp pain in his stomach. He stopped and had a cup of coffee and the pain went away. Thus he continued home.

CHAPTER 12

A MAJOR BEDROOM PROBLEM

A few days later during Drick's daily diabetic injection session, he noticed a small bump on his belly. A week went by; the small bump became larger and started to hurt. Drick touched it and a little blood came out. He thought, 'I am not injecting myself again in the stomach; I will start injecting myself in the thigh.' He loved to eat sweet cakes, even though he was a diabetic and shouldn't, but he always said that we only live once. One day while driving, he noticed a black dot hovering in his eyes. He tried to brush it away, but it remained there.

Drick got home and washed his face, but the dot was not going anywhere. He went into his bedroom and started his daily exercises by lifting some weights, when he observed a bigger red dot in the centre of his right eye.

Drick called his cousin Hazzata Jacobs, who worked in the eye department at the hospital and explained to her what happened. She told him to go right away to the hospital since his diabetes may have started affecting his eyes.

He drove himself to the hospital. When he got there, he explained to the nurses what had happened, and the nurses said,

"You will have to see the doctor immediately."

The doctor disclosed to him that he would have to be doing some laser surgery to break up the blood clots that had formed in his eyes. After the surgery, the doctor said he would be putting Drick into a diabetic clinic because he needed to be monitored better. They gave him some more metformin tablets to use. Drick revealed to the nurse: "I was told by someone that those tablets make you impotent. I have some fine young ladies to take care of!"

The nurse responded. "That's just rumours: they are good for you, and they will help to control your blood sugars. And your fine young ladies, you will be able to take care of them."

Later that day, Drick's friend Kenneth Bovell called him and told him he must drink cod liver oil. "It will help to dissolve the blood in your eyes," so he drank it.

A week later most of the blood was dissolved. Drick thought, 'This is a miracle.' He called one of his young lady friends and asked her if she was free. She said, yes, she would come and visit him at home. This young lady was lovely: her name was Pam. Drick told her to get a cab to his house.

As she arrived he noticed she was wearing an extremely short dress. As she entered the kitchen Drick smiled and licked his lips because he knew he was getting some loving tonight.

Drick cooked some food for Pam and himself, and after they had finished eating, they went to bed. They were kissing and playing with each other for about 15 minutes, when he noticed something was wrong with him: he was not being aroused. 'No, no, no,' he thought, 'this can't be happening to me. I've heard about those damn metformin pills: now they've mashed up my private belongings.'

They continued to play we each other for about 20 minutes more, but nothing happened. Drick made an excuse by saying he wasn't feeling well, then he jumped out of bed and hurried to the bathroom. A few minutes later, Pam got out of bed and went to the bathroom. She knocked on the door and asked Drick if he was okay.

Drick replied, "I don't feel well, I'm just having a little headache."

"Okay no problem," muttered Pam. "I will come back tomorrow evening." Then she left the house and made her way home.

Drick came out of the bathroom minutes later and thought to himself, 'I am finished: I will have to give all my fine young ladies away, what a waste of my life.'

The next day, Drick met up with some of his musician friends at an audition. He asked one of them, "Have you heard about those metformin tablets?"

The friend replied. "Oh no! That tablet will mess your privates up, forget about the girls, it happened to one of my friends. Fortunately, his father knew of some home-made remedy that helped him."

He had to eat a lot of almond nuts, drink almond milk and eat lots of raw spinach: this helped him.

The friend asked Drick, "Why did you ask about those tablets?"

Drick responded. "A friend of mine is getting same problems." It was too embarrassing for him to tell his friend the truth.

Later that day Drick called Pam and cancelled their evening

date, saying he was leaving town for a few weeks. For the next week, Drick cancelled all his meetings and made an appointment to fix his ED problem. He bought 12 boxes of almond drinks, 15 packets of raw almond nuts, and £10 worth of leafed spinach: that was Drick's diet for the whole week.

Five days into his diet while walking down the road he noticed a lady looking at him in a very surprised way, she said, "Please, sir, fix yourself!" Drick looked down and saw a huge, embarrassing bump in his trousers.

"Oops, sorry, madam," he answered. He was thrilled and also embarrassed. Drick was so happy, he hurriedly jumped into his car and went straight home. He rushed into the bedroom and dropped to his knees, thanking the Lord for saving his private parts. He called one of his lady friends, Pam, and said sorry for missing their dinner date, then he asked her to come to his house.

She responded. "I am annoyed with you for cancelling the date."

Drick explained that he had some meeting out of town, and he would make it up to her.

Pam said, "I hope you do not have a headache again."

"No, no, I promise you all my headaches are gone. Get a cab and come over, my dear. I promise you no headaches this time."

Pam got in a cab and made her way to Drick's home.

She loved wearing very short, close-fitting dresses. This turned Drick on right away: his manhood was erected. As Pam entered the house, he grabbed her and rushed her to the bedroom, and hurriedly made love to her.

"Wow!" said Pam as they finished. "That was great. Thank God there were no headaches this time. Oops, look at the time. I've got to rush home to my husband, he is waiting for me. I will call you later." She rushed out of the house.

Drick hurriedly grabbed the phone, and called another one of his ladies and asked her to come over after work.

She said, "Okay. What happened to you for about two weeks? You didn't call me."

Drick pleaded: "I was busy with meetings and other stuff, please come on over, babes, I miss you."

"Okay," she muttered, "I will come after work."

Later that evening, Drick's lady friend came over: her name was Rhian. As she entered, Drick grabbed her and rushed her to the bedroom; he was checking to see if his erection was a one-off. But it was not, so he made passionate love to her.

She whispered, "That was great, I miss you so much, but I have to leave. I've got some kids to look after."

She rushed out of the house. Drick thought, 'What a crazy two weeks in my life. Two weeks ago I couldn't get an erection, then two weeks later I slept with two ladies in one day. My life is like a wave, always going up and down.' He muttered to himself, "Maybe I need to go to church with Mum. I do need to contact her sometime soon, I miss her so much."

CHAPTER 13

MUM GETTING SICK

Drick couldn't sleep: he was tossing and turning, and this caused him to wonder what was happening to him. Minutes later the phone rang: it was his mum. She said, "Drick, it's your mum, I am not feeling well, I got your number from Seri. I would like to see you very soon."

Drick responded. "Okay, Mum, no problem. I do love you. But you know I can't come to London because of my situation, Mum. I have a friend who has a hotel in Derby, and we can meet there, and please don't tell anyone about this trip. From now on, Mum, anytime you're calling me, please don't stay inside the house when you are speaking to me, go outside, because I think your house might be bugged."

"Fine!" uttered Mum. "I will do anything to see my only son," but this made Mum very unhappy, because she couldn't tell anyone, knowing it would have endangered her child's safety.

Drick sent Mum the address of his friend's Hotel, and reminded her, "Don't tell anyone, because he will cancel the trip." The next day, Drick caught the train and went to Derby to meet his mum. Sitting on the train, Drick thought, 'I am extremely happy to see my mum.' As he arrived at the station in Derby, he began looking around and saw Mum sitting in the corner of the train station. Drick dropped his bags and ran over and hugged her: they both started crying, as it was the first time they had seen each other in a while. He quickly grabbed Mum's bag, and they hurried into a cab. Drick gave the driver the address of the hotel they were staying at.

"Son, it's been a long time. I haven't seen you. What has happened to you?"

Drick motioned to his mouth, telling her to be quiet. He responded. "We will speak when we get to the hotel."

They arrived at the hotel and went into their rooms. Mum uttered, "Your sons are missing you so much. Seri told me you got remarried and have another son. I would be the happiest person in the world if you could come home to London." But Mum knew that was not possible.

Drick added, "Let's go to lunch today, and then we'll go to dinner later in the evening." So they went to lunch and in the evening they went to dinner.

After dinner they went back to their hotel room and fell asleep.

At about 4 in the morning Drick heard his mum calling him, and he thought, 'What could she be calling me for at this time?' He looked across the room and saw his mum sitting at the end of the bed, shaking as if someone was pushing her, so he jumped out of bed and grabbed both of her hands. Drick realised she was shaking so violently: this caused him to shake as well, then she said to him, "I don't know what's happening to me, my son."

Drick thought, 'This is very serious, I need to call an ambulance immediately.' Drick grabbed a few pillows and placed them under her legs to elevate them, but this didn't help because she was still shaking vigorously when the ambulance arrived. Drick thought, 'Oh my Lord, please save and help my mum get well.'

The ambulance arrived and the paramedics placed his mum onto a stretcher and took her to the hospital. Mum's shaking had calmed down before she got to the hospital. She uttered, "Take my phone and call my sister please." Mum was an identical twin, and her sister lived in America. Drick took her phone and called her sister.

His Auntie Crisy answered the phone, and recognised his voice immediately and thereafter said, "My nephew, where have you disappeared to all these years?"

Drick answered, "Sorry, Auntie, I was having a few problems, and I didn't want to get anyone involved. Auntie, I'm calling to say Mum is sick, and I just brought her to the hospital." Then Drick put the phone on the loudspeaker setting.

His mum muttered that she didn't know what had happened to her, then they both began crying. Drick questioned Mum: "Why are you guys crying?"

Mum mumbled, "I forgot to tell you your big cousin Gully died."

Drick immediately fell to the floor, screaming, "What!? I saw her months ago: she was helping me get married." Auntie uttered to Mum, "I will call you back later," then she hung up the phone.

Drick was extremely hurt; he tried his best to console himself because he didn't want Mum to worry. Mum tried to console Drick, but she still was not happy about what had happened to her:

she thought she would lose all of her independence and wouldn't be able to go around the country with her friends, and also go to church freely. Mum explained that a few days earlier she fell over, hitting her head, while running for the train to visit a friend.

She also stated that the doctor explained she had tinnitus problems; this had caused her to lose her balance on many occasions. But she didn't know what had caused her to shake so violently. 'Oh no, I've lost my perfect cousin. Now I'm going to lose my mum. What's happening to me?' Drick stepped outside the hospital for a second.

He looked up and saw someone walking towards him; his heart almost stopped for a second because the gentleman had the height and build like Radovan Bloodmic, but it wasn't him. As Drick got into a cab his phone would not stop ringing: all of his family began to call him, because Mum had given his phone number to her sister who sent it to all of her children. The news of Drick's mum being sick travelled very fast. 'All of my cousins in America called, some of them were crying, some were very sad.' One question was common: they all asked Drick why he disappeared; some of them thought he was dead.

He said to them, "It's a long story, and I will tell you when Mum gets well first, then I will let you know what happened." Hours later, after doing some tests on Mum, the hospital found out that Mum had vertigo combined with her tinnitus. She was discharged the next day from the hospital.

They went back to the hotel and spent a couple more weeks there then went home. Drick was looking on the internet for treatment to help Mum get better. Two weeks went by, and Mum started regaining her balance. She was walking with the aid of a walking stick; however, after two weeks she began smiling because she didn't need it anymore.

Augusta knew that she hadn't lost her independence, and she could now go to church without the aid of anyone. 'It's been a scary time,' thought Drick.

I need to hurry up and send Mum back to London, because I need to go back into hiding before the debt collector and the inspector catch me. Drick said to Mum, "I will be seeing you in a couple of months," and placed her on the train to London. Then he caught a train to Cardiff because he was having a meeting in Bristol the next day.

CHAPTER 14

DATING A LADY HALF HIS AGE

Drick had to meet up with some old friends at a studio in Bristol when a lady came in and said, "Hi, Drick, how are you? Do you remember me?"

Drick answered, "Yes, I do, your name is Tia. Lovely Tia, I will always remember you, dear, we were good friends for years."

Tia responded. "I heard you got married then you disappeared."

Drick continued. "How are you and how is your daughter?"

"She's okay, she should be here any minute, she's just buying some things at the shop for her daughter." Tia questioned Drick, "How old are you now? Maybe you are about 44 years old. I do remember you were the same age as me. Do you have any children?"

Drick muttered in a very quiet voice, "Yes I do!" as if he didn't want to mention his kids. "I have two boys, James and James JR."

The conversation was interrupted by a lovely young lady about 5 feet 8 inches tall with a kid about two years old with her. Tia blurted out, "This is my daughter and granddaughter. My daughter's name is Rena, and my granddaughter's name is Stachia."

Drick smiled and responded. "Tia, how old is your daughter?"

Tia announced angrily, "Hey mind your own business!"

Rena disclosed to Drick, "I'm 22 years old and my daughter is two years old. I love this music business, you know. Are you into music?"

Drick answered, "I used to have my own music video studios, and I can help you. Here is my number." Drick reached into his pocket and gave his business card to Rena. Her mum got up and snatch it out of her hands.

Tia burst out, "I need to protect my daughter from vultures like you. She is a bit on the dumb side. She's made one mistake already and I don't want her to make another mistake with anyone in the music industry."

Drick murmured, "It's getting hot in here, I'm going to step outside for a bit. I'll be back."

As Drick stepped outside, Rena got up and implied she was going outside, too, so she quickly went outside, then she slipped Drick her business card and ran back into the studio before her mum observed.

Tia saw Rena come back into the studio smiling. So Tia questioned Rena.

"Where were you?"

Rena answered, "I popped outside for a second, Mum. Why are you asking all these questions, are you the police?"

Tia got very annoyed and vented, "No, no, no, this is not happening again over my dead body!"

Then she got up and angrily exited the studio. She went outside to look for Drick. Tia found him outside on his laptop, and said,

"Excuse me, I need to speak to you about my daughter. I see the way she's looking at you and I can't have her feelings being hurt again by another man."

Drick responded. "Tia, I don't know what you're talking about. I just give your daughter my business card, and that's it."

So Tia turned and went back into the music studio and sat down quietly. Drick returned to the studio and began smiling when he saw Rena. Drick could see under her hat, which she had pulled down in her face, that she was a very beautiful young lady with long legs and beautiful skin, and a captivating smile.

But he could also feel those drilling eyes of Tia on him looking as if she was a bodyguard, hence he sat down quietly for the rest of the music session and uttered nothing.

About 15 minutes went by when Tia got up suddenly and broke the silence.

"We are leaving now. Rena, get my granddaughter and we're going right away!" Afterwards they left. One of the sound engineers muttered to Drick, "Be careful with that woman Tia: she is very crazy and don't mess with her daughter. She is extremely annoyed with the drummer because he is her granddaughter's father, but he is saying the child is not his."

Then the drummer jokingly played a drum roll and everyone in the studio began laughing. Drick got up and said, "You crazy people are getting me into trouble with my friend. I am going home now."

But he could not take Rena out of his mind. She was so beautiful and innocent-looking. As he got home Drick took his dinner and went to bed. The phone rang and it was Rena. She said she could not sleep so she called Drick to speak with him.

Drick asked, "Where is your mum?"

Rena replied, "She is at her home with her granddaughter and I am at my home by myself." She continued. "Do you have a wife or a lady?"

"No!" responded Drick. "Why did you ask?"

Rena continued. "I would like to come to your house tonight to talk about music, I hope it is not too late."

Drick looked at the clock in his room and observed it was showing 10 pm, then he said, "Okay we can speak for an hour, then I have to sleep."

Rena answered, "Okay, I will be there in 20 minutes."

Drick quickly rushed into the bath and showered then got dressed. The doorbell rang, and as Drick opened the door he was shocked because the Rena who was standing in front of him was 10 times more beautiful than when he saw her earlier that day.

Rena walked into the house looking very pretty with close-fitting trousers and top: this outfit showed all the curves and contours on her body. Drick thought, 'That's not the best clothing to wear when you going to have a meeting about music at 10 o'clock at night.'

Rena looked at Drick and mentioned, "Do you like what you see?"

He replied, "Yes, I do like what I see, but I can also see your mum trying to come over here and kill me! You know your mum doesn't like us being in the same room. What will she say if she hears about this meeting?"

Rena declared, "She does not control my life. I am 22 years old, and I am my own woman."

Drick motioned. "Have a seat, and would you like something to drink?"

Rena responded. "Yes please, rum and Coke."

So he gave her the drink, then he asked, "What part of the music business are you interested in?"

Rena responded. "I'm a very good dancer and I can sing." Then she began singing and dancing very seductively. He could see her body slithering like a snake.

Rena questioned Drick, "Do you like it?" then she danced right up in front of Drick.

She smiled and kissed him on the cheek. Drick was surprised and pushed her away, then he mentioned, "I'm sorry but I'm double your age."

"That's not a problem," replied Rena. "Age is nothing but a number and I've been out with older men before."

Drick responded. "This meeting is getting heated real quick, can we slow down a bit?"

"No!" uttered Rena. "I need a man like you: my mum always speaks about how great a man you are. I would like you to be my man."

Rena pushed Drick onto the floor, then she jumped on top of him. One thing led to another, then they began making love.

Drick thought, 'I'm going to be a dead man in at least two weeks because when her mum finds out, it's goodbye for me.' He muttered, "I can't believe I'm now dating a woman half my age!"

About an hour later Rena said she had to leave because she needed to collect her daughter from her mum, then she kissed

Drick and uttered goodnight, and left the house. This continued with them having frequent phone calls; afterwards she began coming at least three times a week to his house.

CHAPTER 15

THE PREGNANCY ACCUSATION

The house phone began ringing, but Drick was scared to pick it up because he had about 7 people seriously looking for him. A second later his mobile phone began to ring: it was his mother. She uttered, "How are you, son? I was speaking to your friend John, who lives in Brighton, and he said to tell you he is still angry with you. What did you do?" questioned Mum.

Drick did not reply: he was so happy to hear his mother's voice, and wanted to know how she was feeling. "Sorry, I have to go now, Mum, my other phone is ringing. Bye." Drick started crying: he really loved his mum. He could hear the other phone ringing. Drick answered the phone.

"Hello who's this?"

"It's me, Tia, Rena's mother. Are you crying?" she asked.

"Yes, I'm just having some problems," uttered Drick.

"Okay!" Tia responded. "I have some more problems for you, Rena is pregnant."

Drick questioned, "Do you have any proof of that, and did she tell you she was pregnant from me?"

Tia burst out, "Yes! It is for you, because you're the type of man who knows how to control a little girl like her." Tia continued. "She's very infatuated by you, and I know she worships you by the way she speaks about you. She's in love with you, and you are her baby's father."

Drick replied, "So is that your only proof?"

Tia responded. "She's getting fat, and has a lot more confidence in the way she is speaking. I'm coming right now to your house, and afterwards we can arrange her wedding because she will not be having a second baby without being married!"

Drick declared, "Tia, don't come to my house because you're not invited."

Tia replied, "Okay, when I get there, you can stop me."

Drick called Rena and remarked, "Rena, you didn't tell me you were pregnant."

She answered, "No, I'm not pregnant. And who said that?" she asked.

Drick blurted out, "Your mother said you are pregnant, and she's coming over here to deal with me."

"Okay! I'll be coming over there, because since I started speaking to you my mum has gone really crazy. She said you guys used to be such good friends. I'm on my way," declared Rena.

The mobile phone began ringing again. Drick answered, "Hello, who's this?"

"Good day, my name is Radovan Bloodmic. May I speak to Drick E Crawford?"

Drick added, "You're speaking to him."

Radovan declared, in his angry Russian accent, "It has been

two years since you have not paid your debt, and you know I don't like being made a fool of. I'll have to teach you a lesson." He hung up the phone.

Drick became petrified, and started rubbing his head vigorously. A few minutes later the door buzzer rang. This scared Drick, so he jumped out of the chair and looked out of the window, and saw it was Tia. Drick thought, 'I am not opening the door for that crazy woman.'

She began screaming and shouting for Drick to come and open the door. To his horror he saw two tinted-out Mercedes Jeeps driving away slowly. 'That must have been Radovan Bloodmic: he was sitting outside looking at the house,' Drick thought. 'I am sure he'll be back.'

The doorbell rang again, so Drick looked angrily through the window, but it was Rena. She said, "Please let me in, Drick." So Drick opened the door, and Rena and Tia came into the house. Rena motioned to her mum.

"Please sit down because we need to speak about this baby you say I'm having for Drick, and who said I was having a baby?"

Tia declared, "I saw you putting on weight, and I found a receipt from Mothercare in your bag."

Rena stressed, "Basically, Mum, do not be looking through my bags, and I'm getting big because of my contraceptive and is that the reason why are you calling Drick, and not speaking to me about me having a baby? He is not your daughter, I am, and what's this got to do with you, and why are you so angry with him?"

"Okay, Rena, I'm sorry but Drick, I still don't like you, because there is something shady about you, and I don't like it."

Drick looked out of his window again and saw the Mercedes Jeeps driving by slowly. Tia looked at Drick and shook her head, saying, "I don't want you near my daughter, but Rena will have to learn. I am sure I heard you were married and had kids."

Rena got off the chair and hugged and kissed Drick, then said to her mother, "Let's go home now, this is the end of this story. I'm not pregnant."

Tia pointed to Drick and declared, "There is something about you I do not like," then they left the house.

CHAPTER 16

A LIFE-THREATENING TEXT

Drick thought, 'Oh what a beautiful day.' When he got out of bed he did his 30 minutes' exercise and checked his diabetes blood sugar levels: they were fine, hence he made breakfast and left the house for his hospital appointment at the diabetic clinic.

When the clinic was finished he got into his car and was on his way to work. Then Drick remembered he had to call a friend, then he reached into his pocket for his phone and to his surprise, the phone was blank because the battery had died. "Oops!" he muttered. "My phone needs charging."

After he arrived at work, he took his battery charger from his drawer and plugged it into the socket.

When the phone was charged he decided to call his friend and arrange a studio session. As he finished his phone call, he noticed there was a text on his phone, saying that his mother was sick and very ill in the hospital. Drick thought, 'I hope I didn't cause my mother illness when I faked my disappearance.' He called the number but got no answer.

Drick became very afraid: he loved his mother so much, considering his situation he had to stay away from her for a while.

Drick was very eager, and would do anything to see his mum, even though he knew that trouble was always around the corner. Drick was thinking about his mother every day since her sickness. He thought, 'What would I do if I lose my mother? It would be a terrible life, living knowing that you killed your mother from grief.' Subsequently he sat there thinking for about 30 minutes. His phone began vibrating. It was a text message with the address of the hospital. Drick thought, 'Something is not right. Why are they sending me the address of the hospital and no name?'

So he went onto his computer and looked into Google Maps. He typed in the address he was sent, although he wasn't surprised to find out this address was a house and not a hospital. The person stated in the text that he must hurry and get there in an hour before anything worse happened to his mum. Drick called a friend and borrowed his car, then he drove to the address, but didn't park the car near the address. Drick thought he would park the car in the street nearby. As he was driving by the address he noticed two Mercedes Jeeps were parked in the street. He kept driving around for about two minutes, then he parked the car in the nearby street. Afterwards he walked to the address and knocked on the door.

As he entered the door he was greeted by two big men each about 6 feet 7 inches tall. They motioned him to come in and have a seat. Sitting in the room was Radovan Bloodmic. One of the doors in the room opened, and out stepped a beautiful blonde lady. She walked towards Drick and uttered, "My name is Michaela Bloodmic, and I'm Radovan's wife."

Everyone in the room began laughing loudly when Radovan

stood up, raising his hands, and declared, "You don't want to mess with her. I should know because I am her husband."

Drick unexpectedly felt a hand on his shoulder, as he was pushed into a chair by Michaela who quickly pulled a needle out of her pocket. One of the tall gentlemen hurriedly went into the room and came back with a box in his hands. Drick could hear a hissing sound coming from the box, he thought, I know this sound, it's a snake! With one swipe, Michaela knocked off the cover of the box and grabbed the snake, sticking the injection needle into its head, extracting out some venom from the back of the neck, then hurled the snake back into the box.

She stepped over to Drick and boosted, "I could paralyse you forever." She began to laugh and stated, "You will be stiff, but not dead for years." Michaela brought they needle close to Drick's face and declared, "I have a few nice cars to buy. When are we going to get our money?"

Suddenly the sound of a police siren could be heard: it became louder and louder. Then two police BMW Jeeps screeched to a halt, and about six armed policemen came towards the house.

However, to Radovan's amazement, they kicked in the neighbours' door, and grabbed the man who was living there, then rapidly pushed him to the floor with guns placed on his back.

Radovan got out of the chair and went to the window. He looked outside and stated to Drick, "I thought it was you who called the police on me." Drick did not reply. He noticed everyone was distracted, so he quickly got up and rushed towards the door. He hurried outside, then began calmly walking past the policemen and uttered, "What's happening?"

The police mentioned the man on the ground: he was a wanted terrorist from the London bombings. Drick walked towards his car because he knew that Radovan would not harm him while the police were there, due to the fact that they were so many armed police around. Afterwards he jumped into his car and was about to drive away when he noticed in the rear-view mirror two black Mercedes Jeeps driving towards the car. He then laid himself flat in the car seat, so he could not be seen by the persons in the Jeeps. He paused for about five minutes then drove off when he was sure no one was following him. He stopped at a traffic light, when to his surprise he pulled up behind the two Mercedes Jeeps.

Drick began to muttering his prayers now that this was the end of him. He thought, 'God, please could you help me?' when, out of the blue, Radovan had emerged from the convoy.

He was walking towards Drick's car, when there was a sudden tap on his window. He turned to his left and noticed it was the police. Drick believed God had answered his prayers. Then he heard a second knock: it was the police telling him he was holding up the traffic.

Suddenly, Drick slumped over his steering wheel as the car shot forward, crashing into the back of one of the Mercedes Jeep. The armed policeman jumped back, drawing his gun from its holster as he jumped back. The other officers all emerged from their vehicles with their guns drawn. They realised what had happened. They opened the door of the car. Drick was still slumped over the steering wheel. He quickly pressed the button on his radio and called for an ambulance.

Radovan noticed what had happened and shouted, "Is he okay, Officer?"

The police responded. "No, I think he fainted."

Radovan walked towards the back of the Jeep then looked and declared, "Officer, everything is okay here, I will be leaving now."

"No!" responded the officer. "We need to get your details before you leave."

Another officer who was helping collected Radovan's details.

Radovan declared, "Thank you, Officers," as the two Mercedes Jeeps sped away.

Seconds later the ambulance arrived, and Drick had started recovering consciousness. As the paramedic and the police took Drick out of the car, and placed him onto the stretcher, they took him to the hospital where they'd found that his diabetes sugar count was 22. This was extremely high due to Drick spending hours without taking any medication or eating food. He thought, 'That text could have killed me in many ways.' While lying on the hospital bed, Drick was thinking about his mother again. He was considering that being in the hospital had reminded him of her. 'I hope my mum's well,' then he called her to see if she was fine.

CHAPTER 17

FIGHTING IN THE SHOP

The next day, Drick was finishing his producers' meeting when the phone rang. He answered it, and a female voice uttered, "It's me, Madonna."

"Hi, my darling," responded Drick. "I was coming to see you this evening after my meeting at about 10 o'clock. Are you going to be free?"

She uttered, "Yes! I will be wearing my best lingerie for you, so hurry and get here, and bring me some food, please."

"Okay," he added, "I will come and see you when the meeting is finished."

Drick hung up the phone and laughingly announced to his producer colleagues, "I am going to be making love until tomorrow morning!" They all laughed and remarked that Drick was a fortunate man.

The meeting finished at about 10 pm. Drick hurriedly jumped into his car and rushed to Madonna's house. Just as he got inside the house, she observed his hands were empty.

"You forgot what I asked you for. I wanted you to get me some food when you were coming home."

Drick responded. "Oh no, I forgot, let me go and get us the food."

Madonna responded. "Don't worry."

Drick whispered, "I have to keep my promises, so I will go back and get us the food. It won't be long. It's about 20 minutes' drive."

"Don't forget to get me a chicken meal, and do you want me to come with you?" asked Madonna.

"No!" replied Drick. "Don't be afraid: no woman will kidnap me."

Drick got into his car, and drove for about five minutes. He noticed there was a small chicken shop but he didn't like its look, so he decided not to stop there. He continued to McDonald's, because they did much better chicken meals. As he got to the McDonald's drive-through, the line was extremely long. At that point he drove to the Kentucky Fried Chicken (KFC): they had a long line as well. Drick told himself, 'I will have to go back to that small chicken shop because there is no other alternative. I would not say I like their meals, but Madonna loves chicken meals, and I promised to get it for her.' So he parked the car and went to the cashpoint, got some money out, and then went into the chicken shop. As Drick walked into the chicken shop he was greeted by loud laughter: they were a few drunk people, and they we're eating chicken meals. Minutes later they finished and began leaving the shop.

Moments later, one of the ladies from the group came running back into the shop saying she had lost her bag with all her money. She began to look for her purse when a young lady who was in the shop asked her, "Is that the bag on your shoulder you're looking for?"

She mumbled, "Sorry," due to the fact that she had the bag on her shoulder all of the time.

As they were leaving the shop, one of her friends noticed Drick and he burst out, "I remember you: personally you got me locked up in prison a few months ago. Because I was trying to get a music contract and had to attack one of your studio engineers. I recollected he was being rude." He continued. "I recalled you being in the courts telling lies against me, and you were the reason I went to prison."

"There are no cameras here, and you cannot hide. What are you going to do about that?" This made Drick very angry, and so he threw the food he was holding across the counter, and spoke.

"What was that you mentioned?" He stepped towards them.

Drick declared, "If you're a man of the street, touch me and see what will be the outcome."

The man boasted, "I will be calling some of my friends, so I can bust your face in."

When Drick punched him in the face, at that point he pushed him towards the ground. Afterwards he jumped on the man's body while punching him in the head. The man's friends saw what was happening, and the other man and the two ladies all joined in. They jumped onto Drick, and began kicking and punching him. He managed to get up and grabbed a bottle that was on one of the tables and broke it on the edge of the counter, but when the women saw that Drick was extremely serious about stabbing one of them, the women started screaming, "I'm getting out of here he's trying to kill us."

The gentleman who owned the chicken shop begged Drick. "Please, Mister, don't break my shop up."

Drick responded. "I only came here to purchase a chicken meal, boss, for my girlfriend, not to break up your shop. May I purchase another chicken meal please? The first meal is all over your walls. Sorry about that."

Drick took his phone from his pocket and called a couple of his friends, who stated they were in the next street. Minutes later they came into the shop.

They asked Drick what had happened. He explained to his friends that he was buying a chicken meal and got attacked by two women and two men, but the attackers had left. So Drick and his friends began laughing at the incident and sat down waiting for the chicken meal to be cooked. Suddenly two of Drick's attackers came running back into the shop with pieces of metal bars in their hands. One of Drick's friends who was a kung fu expert upturned a table and broke their metal legs off. The metal legs were now used as weapons. In a jiffy, it became a massive fight considering there were people, metal and fried chicken flying through the air. People were getting smacked by metal bars and pushed into the chicken cases, which caused fried chicken to fall everywhere like rain.

The women ran out of the shop and came back in with bottles and threw them, but they missed everyone. One of Drick's friends called some more of his friends to the shop; two cars pulled up. Four men emerged and ran into the shop, then a bigger fight began. The fight ended when one of Drick's friends pulled out a gun from his pocket and started shooting repeatedly into the roof of the shop.

On that account everyone got scared and ran out, including the shop owners. But Drick could not escape because he was pinned under some broken tables. Hence the police came and found Drick on the floor under a pile of tables. They placed him into handcuffs and took him down to the station where he spent almost four hours.

Then police came to the cell and uttered, "Mr. Crawford, someone has bailed you out." To his surprise, it was Madonna.

She declared, "Drick, I only asked you to go and get me a chicken meal. What you did, you and your friends, you decided to start World War 3. I'm still waiting for my chicken meal. Drick, let's get out of here."

They began to leave the police station when Drick noticed the famous two Mercedes Jeeps parked outside the station.

But to his surprise, Radovan was standing laughing and joking with Inspector Earl Killhill. As a result he hurried back into the police station, leaving from a different exit. Madonna looked at Drick and commented, "Why are you behaving so funny? You look like you're hiding from someone very dangerous."

Drick thought, 'Yes, they are dangerous, but right now I'm feeling a bit dizzy. I will need to go to the hospital sometime soon.'

They jumped into her car, and she drove him to her house. While Drick was sitting in Madonna's house he was thinking, 'Oh my God, my life keeps getting worse. Now the detective inspector and the Russian mafia debt collector are ganging up to catch me. I am sure this is the end of me.'

CHAPTER 18

THE HOSPITAL SHOOTING

One Sunday morning Drick got up did his indoor exercises, then made breakfast and decided to go to the park to do some outdoor exercises. As he got to the park, it was about 10 am and the park was almost clear. He started to do some jogging when three guys who were also in the park looked over and saw Drick. When one of them recognised Drick and shouted, "That's him there! I had a fight with him in a chicken shop, let's bust him up."

'Oh no,' thought Drick, 'here we go again.' The guys ran over to Drick, and a fight started: all three of the guys were trying to knock him out.

Drick did boxing when he was younger, so he stepped towards them and knocked out two of the guys, the third one ran off and called the police. A few minutes later an ambulance and police car came. A bystander had seen the fight and also called the police.

The police walked over to Drick and questioned him about what was happening. Drick explained that he came to the park to do some exercises then these three guys jumped him. The third one blurted, "No, we were sitting on the bench and he jumped us from behind and tried to knock all of us out." Suddenly Drick became unwell, and started feeling dizzy; a female officer motioned him to have a seat on the bench, then she assisted him to sit down. As she removed her hand from his back she observed blood.

"Oh no!" she declared. "You've been hurt." At that point she lifted his shirt and looked at this back, then she saw what appeared to be a knife wound. She revealed, "You've been stabbed," so she called for another ambulance. Thereafter Drick fainted: the ambulance came and took him to the hospital.

As he awoke looking around, he questioned, "Where am I?"

One of the nurses responded. "You're in the hospital because you were stabbed, and your diabetes blood count was extremely high, it was 22."

"Oh no!" Drick exclaimed. "That was too high."

"The doctor stated that he needs for you to stay in the hospital for about two weeks, because your blood count is too high and your stab wounds are very deep."

A week went by, when Drick got a phone call. It was his mother: she asked him how he was feeling. He lied and told her he was okay. She reported, "These two men keep calling me every day and asking if I have seen or heard from you. They were even offering money to me if I should see you to call them. One of them was that guy Earl Killhill, the detective inspector, and the other was a funny-speaking guy. I think he was Russian, and his name, Radovan Bloodmic."

"Mum, be careful," uttered Drick. "They probably have your house bugged so they can hear all your calls."

Mum declared, "I love you, son." Then she hung up the phone.

The phone rang again, and this time it was a familiar voice. "Hi, I heard you got stabbed and are in the hospital."

Drick responded. "Who is this?"

"It's me, Rena. My mum states she's sorry, she wasn't the person that stabbed you. She still doesn't like you, but I do love you. Please send me the hospital address, and I will be coming to see you."

Drick uttered, "Someone's trying to call me," so he put Rena on hold. Then he answered the phone. "Hello, good day, this is Drick."

"It's me, Earl Killhill. Did you see that guy Radovan? He knows where you are and is coming to get you. I think he's going to kill you, and I will be at the hospital in five minutes. I heard he bought some guns, and that bastard has double-crossed me."

Drick thought, 'The last time I saw the detective and the debt collector, they were laughing and having a very good time. Life is like a wave, it's always going up and down, and you can't predict anything. Yesterday they were friends, today their bitter enemies. I'm discharging myself out of this hospital right now.'

As Drick tried to get his clothing, in walked the detective inspector and some of his colleagues; some of them were heavily armed as if they were ready for an all-out war. The inspector stated, "Put on your clothing, Drick, we are leaving this hospital right now."

"Okay," replied Drick as he put on his clothing. The doors of the ward flung open and in walked Radovan Bloodmic and two of his henchmen; they also were heavily armed, and walked directly towards Drick, and revealed to the inspector, "I'm taking him today."

The inspector responded, "Over my dead body."

Radovan stated, "Okay, if I don't have him, no one will get him!" Then he started shooting.

The detective and his colleagues returned fire. Drick was lying under a hail of bullets. He could hear patients screaming, and bullets whizzing by him. He could also hear Radovan and the inspector shouting insults at each other.

'Everyone wanted to take me, now they're prepared to kill themselves over me. Life is like a wave: it's always going up and down.' Everyone could hear loud sirens heading towards the hospital, and Radovan knew the inspector had called for backup.

He looked to his left, then to his right, and at that point he noticed one of his henchmen had been shot dead. Drick thought, 'I better get out of here before all those policemen get here,' so he jumped to his feet and ran towards the door. Before he could run through the door, the inspector shot him in the left arm, but he managed to drag himself out of the door and disappeared.

The inspector never followed him because he wanted to keep the patients in the hospital and himself safe. Thus he let Radovan and his colleague escape. Thereafter the Inspector took Radovan's dead colleague down to the hospital morgue.

Drick was whisked away immediately by Inspector Earl Killhill: he told him he would have to go into hiding, because Radovan could get me. Drick turned to the inspector and expressed, "Thanks very much but I wouldn't trade my freedom with no one, not even Radovan. I think I'm too clever for him to catch me, and I have God on my side, and He will protect me always. My mum stated that she always prays for me. Also I do believe that I am protected by the great man above. He is not ready for me so I will have to turn you down on your offer. Thanks for protecting me today, but I think I'm okay. My life is always going up and down."

Drick walked out of the hospital and jumped into a cab and went home. He thought, 'I have to move again because Radovan will stop at nothing to get me. I will move to Leeds because one of my new friends, Patrice Jacobs, lives there.'

CHAPTER 19

WINNING THE LOTTERY

While in Leeds Drick decided to take a trip to Bradford to meet a friend. Whilst on his journey, he was driving along a street, when he observed that his car required petrol. He pulled into the petrol station. Drick asked the station attendant if they sold scratch cards. The station attendant replied, "No, sir." He pointed and said, "The newsagent on the corner sells lottery tickets."

Drick left his car at the petrol station and walked to the shop. He went into the shop and asked if they had any scratch cards for sale. The salesman behind the counter said, "No, but if you want you can buy some lottery tickets instead."

"Oh no, I never win anything," Drick uttered. Placing his hand into his pocket, he observed they was some change in them.

"Let me try my luck: my life can't get any worse than it already is, it can only get better."

At that moment he purchased a few lottery tickets, and went back to get his car from the petrol station. Drick got into the car and continued his journey to his friend's house in Bradford, then he left a few hours later and went back home to Leeds.

As he arrived home, Drick took off his clothing and placed

them into the washing machine, then he turned on the washing machine and started washing his clothing, then went to bed. About half an hour later he jumped out of bed in a hurry and ran swiftly towards the kitchen. Hastily he opened the door of the washing machine. Drick quickly took out the trousers he had been wearing and searched through their pockets: there were no lottery tickets. He thought, 'How could I have been so stupid?' Then he took out his shirt and found that there was a plastic bag in one of its pockets. Then he remembered putting the lottery tickets into the plastic bag, so he quickly opened the bag and found the lottery tickets in it. Luckily, no water had got into the plastic bag.

Drick placed the tickets onto his glass table and stated, "I will never forget these tickets again." He was even more excited about finding the lottery tickets. So he cancelled all his plans for Saturday evening, saying, "I'm feeling lucky. I'm going to sit in front of the television and look at the lottery on Saturday being drawn." Saturday came, and Drick sat in front of the television with a box of popcorn and a can of beer.

This was all new to him, because every Saturday evening he was out partying. The time came for the lottery to be drawn. As the first number was called Drick laughed and uttered, "Oh great, I have at least one number. The second and third number were called." Drick became overwhelmed with joy because at least he had three numbers now. When the fourth number was called Drick started shaking, then the fifth number was called. Instantly Drick recognised that he was one number from winning the lottery. The pressure was too much for Drick. He started to cry, because he recognised he only needed the bonus number 10. He muttered, "Oh Lord, please make the bonus number be 10." The next number was called and it was number 10. Drick was stunned for about 30 seconds. He started shaking, then crying and screaming, due to the fact that his life was changed forever.

Standing up, he began punching himself, thinking that it might be a dream, but it was not. Thinking it was some kind of prank, he didn't know anyone at the shop where he had bought the lottery tickets from.

Then Drick went onto the internet and double-checked the numbers, and to his surprise they were all correct. He muttered to himself, "I will call all my friends and let them know I won the lottery. Oh no," he muttered to himself, then he decided against it because all of his friends will tell other friends, then his enemies will know, and they will be coming for their money.

"I think I will call my mum," but he didn't have her phone number, because he had lost his phone. Just then his phone rang: it was his mum. It was as if she was psychic and read his mind.

Drick's mum said, "Hello, son, it's me, your mother."

Drick announced, "Mum, I'm thrilled to hear your voice. My life will be going back to normal soon, and you will see me every day."

Mum responded. "I just called to see how you were, my son. I was looking at the lottery being drawn on the TV a few minutes ago, when I checked my lottery tickets not one number was called. I heard some lucky person somewhere won all that £15 million."

Drick couldn't believe his ears. He whispered, "How much money, Mum?"

She repeated, "£15 million. I wish it was my son or me."

Mum declared. "Son, why are you not speaking? Did you win the lottery?"

Drick was quiet for a few seconds then he muttered, "Yes, Mum, I won the lottery."

Mum declared, "The first thing you need to do is say your prayers, son. Then second you will thank the Lord for winning, and the third thing you need to do is to stop those two men from calling me every day of my life. We are going to church tomorrow and I will be catching the train tonight in an hour and coming to Leeds."

Mum arrived that evening. Thus the next day, Drick and Mum got dressed and went to the nearest church.

Drick warned Mum before they got into the church: "Please do not tell anyone that I won the lottery." Mum agreed because she was so happy to be in his presence again.

Sunday evening Drick and his mum travelled back to London. Drick went to the lottery headquarters, and presented his winning ticket: he was told that he would not have all the money at one time. "You can only have 5 million and the other 10 million will be in instalments." Instantly Drick agreed, and left his bank details for the money to be transferred into his account. Not to his surprise, he observed one Black Mercedes Jeep parked in the lottery headquarters car park.

Therefore he boldly walked over to the Jeep that Radovan was sitting in. Today, to Drick's surprise, Radovan Bloodmic was extremely friendly, and happy to see him: it was as if he knew Drick had won the lottery. He greeted him as if they were friends for years.

Drick stated, "I would not be able to give you the full £5 million, but I can give you 3 million and the remainder will be paid in instalments."

"Okay," Radovan responded. "It has been years, and you never paid any money, so I will accept your offer. I will also make a contract, and you must sign it. I want to have my instalments every month."

Drick declared, "Please don't be following me and my family around anymore: you've been doing this for years."

Radovan stated, "I only needed to collect my money, now that I have some money I will stop following you around."

Drick thought, 'The next people I need to speak to is the Department for Works and Pensions and Revenue.' Hence he called the Revenue Department and a lovely young lady answered. Drick explained that his accountant had disappeared and didn't pay his taxes. The young lady responded, "I will call you back in 20 minutes, then we make the total calculation."

About half an hour later the young lady from the Revenue Department called Drick, and backdated the outstanding balance: it was £900,000. Drick was quiet for a moment, because he knew the last time he spoke to someone in the Revenue Department they gave him a quote much higher than that. Therefore he asked again, "Are you sure?"

The young lady uttered, "Yes, I'm sure. I will send you over an email with the total breakdown."

Drick inquired, "Can I make payments in instalments? I will try my best to pay this off in six months."

He knew now he would have constant lottery money coming into his account. The young lady agreed and stated, "I will send you the confirmation and contract by email."

Drick muttered, "Now I can walk freely on the road. Four days ago my life seemed like hell, I was always running and looking over my shoulder. And four days later it seems like heaven. My life is like a wave: it goes up and comes down."

CHAPTER 20

DRICK GETTING HIS LIFE BACK

Drick thought, 'I will be getting my nice way of life back, the same life I lived years ago before I started gambling and made a mess of my life. I will never be going into any casinos again, getting caught living a carefree life. I am not taking any more chances in life because taking chances put me in debt, even though taking chances took me out of debt, and gave my life back to me. That's it, I'm not taking another chance. I have to be a bit more responsible, or my life will become hell again. Just then the phone rang: it was Drick's mum.

"Your old house was up for sale, at half the normal price, the reason being its owner is leaving the country." Augusta questioned, "Do you want me to speak to them because Stacey goes to my church?"

"Okay," uttered Drick, "speak to them please, Mum. Also give it all your blessing. I think It would be nice to go back to Greenwich and live in my old home."

"Okay," responded Mum. "Let me go now and try to see if I can speak to Stacey. It would be nice to get it for a quarter of the price."

Drick laughed and stated, "This is not shopping in the market, Mum, this is buying a house."

Mum stated, "I will go now, and I'll call you tomorrow."

The next day Mum called and declared that they would be accepting an offer for at least £200,000, because they're leaving the country in a few weeks.

Drick responded to Mum, "It will not be a problem. I will call my bank manager and make the necessary arrangements to transfer the money into their account," Drick begged. "Please let them know I'm interested and don't take any more offers. I will be buying the house as soon as possible. I am free now, Mum. I can live in London."

Mum continued. "Do you know I'm still in contact with Seri?"

"Yes, Mum! I do know you are still in contact with her. You love her like a daughter, and you wouldn't let her go especially now."

Drick uttered, "I heard Diane sent James Jr to live with you. I always knew that woman was only pretty, Thus now you are even happier having both of your grandchildren there with you."

Mum announced, "Seri is single now, because her husband got fed up of her. Thus every morning she wakes up she's crying for you."

Drick started laughing.

Mum replied, "That was not funny. Her husband had to leave her, and I agree with him, because Seri was crying to me every day about you."

So a week went by when Drick's bank manager called him with the confirmation of the deal.

Drick called Mum, and told her the deal was a success and stated, "Mum, I love you, and I will be moving back to London to live near you, in a week or two."

Mum was overwhelmed and declared, "You have to start going to church every Sunday."

Drick muttered, "Mum, you're pushing it."

Mum responded. "Have you called and told those two men to stop following me around?"

"Yes, I did!" replied Drick. "I called and made arrangements with the Russian man, and he will stop following us around."

"And the other man, what happened to him? And what about the Inspector, I think his name was Earl?"

Drick answered, "I will call him after I am finished speaking to you, because I have spoken to the Revenue Department, and they said everything was okay."

Mum continued. "That is the reason why I told you, son, you need to come to church. Thus you had to disappear from your mum, wives, kids, jobs and hide from these two men for years."

Augusta uttered, "You will be going to church with me from now on."

"Okay!" replied Drick to his mum, then he hung up the phone. He was just about to call the detective inspector when the phone rang again. He said, "Hello, this is Drick E Crawford."

A female voice on the other end said, "Hello, Mr. Crawford, It's me, Seri. I was once Mrs. Crawford. I spoke to Mum, and she announced you will be coming back to live in Greenwich. Is it true, and can I come with the kids to see you?"

Drick replied, "Yes that's not a problem. I'll be happy to see you and them. I hope you're not planning to beat me up again."

"No!" Seri replied. "I will not be beating you up, this time I'll be bringing both of your sons, James Jr and James Crawford Sr, with me to see you. I will be coming sometime this week."

The week went by: it seemed like a long time. So Drick told his friends in Leeds thank you very much for everything they had given him, but he needed to go back to London where he needed to be with his mum, wife and kids.

A week went by. Drick packed and moved from Leeds to London. He arranged to meet Mum at the house. Mum came over as arranged, and she was delighted.

"I've always loved coming to this house when you were and weren't here. That's the main reason why I made friends with Stacey, because I always hoped and prayed that one day my son would be back in this house, even though I thought it was a dream. Today it became a reality. Today is a special day, because I'm back in the house with my son who owns it."

They were interrupted by the doorbell. Mum hurried to the door.

Drick asked, "Mum, did you invite someone here?"

"Yes!" she replied. "Some people very special to us."

Mum opened the door and two boys, one about ten years old, the other about two years old, rushed to her and said, "Grandma," and behind them walked a lady.

Drick recognised her instantly, and started smiling because it was his first wife, Seri. She smiled and rushed over to Drick then hugged and kissed him. Then two men stepped into the house after his ex-wife with suitcases. They placed them on the floor and rushed out of the door as if there was much more luggage to be brought into the house.

Then Mum said, "Let me go outside and help bring in the other suitcases."

"What, another suitcase?!" Drick questioned.

Mum responded: "The suitcases that belong to the kids." Then she continued. "Come and help me, and stop asking silly questions, son."

Drick smiled and said nothing because he knew this was exactly what his mum was planning, all because she loved her grandchildren. Drick went outside and saw Mum struggling with two suitcases, then he took them from her and uttered, "Mum, go and relax, I will help them bring the suitcases inside." So she smiled and kissed him. She declared, "I love you, even though you have been to hell and back. But while you were in hell, I was always praying for you to be back."

Drick stated, "Mum, could I have a word with you please? What exactly did you plan as I got here? You moved Seri and the kids back into the house. I think I can make my own decisions. You know, Mum."

"Yes, my son," replied Mum. "I know what's best for you: you need to have your kids with you always. Because I brought you up without a father, and I want all my grandchildren to live close to me."

Drick knew it was okay by him for his children and his ex-wife to move into the house, but he wanted to do it himself, not having his mum force it upon him.

Then Mum rudely replied, "Do you want me to ask them to leave?"

"No!" replied Drick. "I am happy. I have my mum, children, my love, and my life back again. Thank you, Mum: that's the reason I have booked a one-month holiday for all of us to go to Barbados, because I have plenty of money now."

Drick booked a large holiday for his family because it was years since they were together. Two weeks later they all got on a plane from Gatwick to Barbados for their holiday where there was no running or hiding: it was all sun, sand and sea.

THE END